SHADOW SCHOOL

PHANTOMS

Also by J. A. White

Nightbooks

The Thickety Series
A Path Begins
The Whispering Trees
Well of Witches
The Last Spell

Shadow School Series
Archimancy
Dehaunting
Phantoms

J. A. WHITE

SHADOW SCHOOL

PHANTOMS

 KATHERINE TEGEN BOOKS
An Imprint of HarperCollins Publishers

Katherine Tegen Books is an imprint of HarperCollins Publishers.

Shadow School #3: Phantoms
Copyright © 2021 by J. A. White

Library of Congress Control Number: 2020952883
ISBN 978-0-06-283834-6

Typography by Andrea Vandergrift
21 22 23 24 25   PC/LSCH   10 9 8 7 6 5 4 3 2 1
❖
First Edition

For Brad,
the smartest guy I know
and a fellow ghost fan

CONTENTS

Through the Mirror

C ordelia Liu settled into her usual spot and waited for a ghost to appear.

All was silent and still. That would change in twenty minutes, when the buses arrived and unloaded their daily cargo of students, but for now Shadow School felt like her own private world. It was nice. Comforting. But not the way it used to be. Cordelia missed the thrill of figuring out a Brightkey, the pure bliss when she sent a spirit into its Bright.

She missed being needed.

Last year, her brilliant friend Agnes had built a machine called a dehaunter, which drew spirits to the mirror gallery and sent them into their Brights without Cordelia doing a single thing. She should have been thrilled. Yet instead of finding a new hobby that didn't threaten her life on a regular basis, Cordelia kept returning to the gallery several mornings a week, hoping to see a ghost depart so she could capture its face in her sketchbook. She couldn't help the spirits of Shadow School anymore, but at least she could memorialize them. It was better than nothing.

Cordelia drew her knees to her chest and gazed at her surroundings. They had removed the black curtains that once covered the mirrors, exposing the impressive craftsmanship of their frames: wrought iron pounded into autumnal leaves, chestnut filigreed with scenes from a forgotten fairy tale, a circle of crushed sea glass. No two mirrors were alike, though all seemed to hint at a mysterious history best shared by candlelight. Cordelia supposed the same thing could be said about the girl reflected in their surfaces: a stubborn set to the chin, dark eyes aged by secrets far greater than any thirteen-year-old should know—and koala earrings, because koalas were adorable.

The morning wasted away, ghostless. Cordelia removed a thermos of milk tea from her backpack and allowed its creamy sweetness to stave off the morning chill. Shadow School was cold in the winter, as could only be expected from a drafty old mansion, but the temperature drop in the mirror gallery was unusually extreme. Agnes believed that the continual opening and shutting of Bright portals wore away the "preternatural insulation" between the worlds, like an overused window with a cracked seal, and planned to design a series of experiments to test her hypothesis. Cordelia made sure to dress in layers.

She was on her second cup of tea when a man floated into the gallery, his boots hovering inches above the floor.

He didn't seem to mind being pulled by the invisible force of the dehaunter. Indeed, there was a look of pleasant expectation on his face, as though he were a vacationer riding a moving walkway to his flight. Cordelia dug her sketchbook and pencil out of her backpack, nearly knocking over her thermos in the process, and flipped past a parade of ghosts before finding a blank page. She followed the new arrival across the gallery, already drawing. *Early fifties or so. Bump in bridge of nose—broken at some point? Wisp of hair covering bald patch.* Cordelia recorded a general outline of his face with a few rough lines, trying to memorize as many of the details as possible so she could finish the drawing later. The important thing was to work as quickly as possible. If the dehaunter was on its game

3

today, she only had a minute or two.

The ghost came to rest before an odd-shaped mirror whose frame had been fitted together from the bones of a large animal. Cordelia felt a tingling along the tips of her hair as the mirror turned black. This new surface had a liquid quality, like molten shadows. Not for the first time, Cordelia wondered what would happen if she stuck her hand into the portal, though she had no intention of doing so. Even *her* curiosity had its limits.

"There's nothing to be afraid of," Cordelia said, giving the ghost a supportive smile. "You'll be out of here before you know it."

The man ignored her, his attention riveted to the mirror as it cycled through possible Brights, searching for the perfect fit. Sky-high Christmas tree surrounded by carolers? Lake house, blue sky, hammock? Blur of race cars, revving engines, squealing tires?

Out of habit, Cordelia found herself examining the dead man in an attempt to figure out his Brightkey. Before the dehaunter, this was how she had freed the ghosts—by finding the one special object that would unlock their Bright. Each ghost's appearance was designed to give her all the clues she needed. A sauce-splattered T-shirt, for example, might indicate the need for an apron, a napkin, or perhaps one last slice of pizza. The Brightkey for a girl wearing a red cloak might be a book of fairy tales or a basket of bread.

Cordelia had loved solving these little mysteries.

That was over now.

There were no clues to be found in the man before her, nothing special about his appearance at all. This had become the norm since the dehaunter took over. Cordelia supposed it made sense. Shadow School did everything for a reason, and now that the dehaunter was doing such a stupendous job, her help was no longer required.

It made her feel more useless than ever.

She heard the approach of clacking heels and turned to see Dr. Roqueni, the principal of Shadow School, enter the mirror gallery. With her slacks, blazer, and silk blouse, she looked more like a CEO than the principal of a New Hampshire public school. The teal frames of her glasses matched her outfit perfectly.

Dr. Roqueni eyed the ghost uneasily as she crossed the room, giving it a wide berth.

"You shouldn't stand so close," she said.

"He's harmless."

"He *seems* harmless. You can't trust them."

Cordelia took a diplomatic step back. Dr. Roqueni had grown skittish around the ghosts since being possessed last year, and Cordelia didn't want to upset her.

The principal looked down at the drawing pad.

"There are other things to sketch, you know. Trees. Mountains. The living."

Cordelia shrugged.

"Mr. Keene was just talking the other day about how talented you are," Dr. Roqueni continued. "He says he offered to help you build a portfolio so you can skip to the advanced courses when you start high school next year. He's disappointed you haven't taken him up on it."

"I'll talk to him soon."

"Only so much 'soon' left. It's already January. Graduation will be here before you know it. You have a gift, Cordelia. Don't waste it."

"Yeah," Cordelia replied with a meaningful look at the ghost. "The last thing I'd want to do is waste any of my natural gifts."

A smile broke across the ghost's face as the mirror finally settled on a Bright he liked: a college campus with ivy-covered stone buildings and groups of students going from class to class. The ghost stepped through the portal. Cordelia had just enough time to see him stride away, a young man now, with a bookbag over one shoulder, and then the campus was replaced by her reflection. The mirror was just a mirror again.

Dr. Roqueni's shoulders relaxed.

"Have to run," Cordelia said, flipping her sketchbook shut. "Field trip today. Speaking of which—I did some research. Did you know that Gideon's Ark is haunted?"

"Of course I did. By a totally harmless ghost who hasn't been seen in over a year. That's the only reason I okayed the field trip in the first place. Plus it's a fascinating place. Strange, but fascinating."

"Maybe I'll see the ghost," Cordelia said.

Dr. Roqueni gave a long sigh.

"We've been over this a thousand times," she said. "Your Sight only works inside Shadow School."

"You just said yourself that the ghost hasn't been seen in over a year. Which means, at some point, someone saw him."

"A momentary glimpse. A tear in the fabric. Not true Sight."

"It's not impossible, though. Elijah Shadow could see ghosts anywhere."

"He was a rare exception. If you could see ghosts everywhere you went, don't you think you would have noticed by now?"

"Maybe not. Ghosts aren't exactly 'everywhere.'"

She had certainly looked hard enough, though. For the past six months, Cordelia had pestered her parents into taking her to every haunted landmark in the area. The Mount Washington Hotel. The Three Chimneys Inn. Cordelia had even dragged them to multiple ghost tours in Boston and Salem.

She loved her parents, and spending time with them had been fun. But she hadn't seen a single ghost.

"You've already done enough," Dr. Roqueni said. "These spirits will never be trapped again. Isn't that what really matters? At last, they'll be able to move on." She placed her hands on Cordelia's shoulders and looked deeply into her eyes. "You might want to follow their lead. You'll be a high school student in just a few months. It's time to develop more appropriate interests."

"Can I bring the spectercles on the field trip?" Cordelia asked.

Dr. Roqueni threw up her arms. "For goodness' sake. You're relentless."

"Just as an experiment. They let people without the Sight see ghosts, right? And since they work in Shadow School, it makes sense they might work outside—"

"Enough," Dr. Roqueni said. She had switched to her principal voice, which was capable of quieting down an entire lunchroom with a few well-enunciated words. "Listen to me. You should never seek ghosts out on purpose. They're *dangerous*. When are you finally going to understand that, Cordelia Liu?"

The morning bell rang.

"I have to go," Cordelia said, grabbing her bag.

"The buses leave first thing after homeroom."

"Can you stay after school today? I have a bit of news. I wanted everyone to be there."

"Sure. I'll tell Benji and Agnes."

"Thanks. Think about what I said. And *no spectercles.* Just enjoy the trip like a normal kid for once."

"All right. See you later!"

Cordelia ran out of the gallery. The metal cases that housed the spectercles clinked together in her bag.

Gideon's Ark

After a nausea-inducing trip along a winding mountain road, Cordelia was thrilled to finally escape the bus. She flipped up the hood of her red woolen coat and followed the stream of students into the frigid January wind. Most kids were already snapping pics of their unusual destination: a wooden ark as large as a cruise ship, sitting on the edge of the mountain.

"Ah, Shadow School," said Benji, following Cordelia down the steps of the bus, "where even the field trips are weird."

"That's a big boat," said Cordelia.

"It's not a boat," said Agnes, exiting the bus behind Benji. "Boats float. Look at that hull! It's not nearly wide enough to generate the buoyant force necessary for a ship of that size to remain above water."

"Does having so much stuff in your head ever make it hurt?" Benji asked.

"Nope. Just stupid questions." Agnes rubbed her temples. "Ow!"

"Keep moving, eighth graders!" shouted Mr. Derleth, ushering them across the parking lot. It was empty except for a row of vehicles that probably belonged to the employees: a few cars, a white van, and a pickup truck with too many bumper stickers. The students merged onto a path squeezed tight by rounded piles of snow. Rock salt crunched beneath their boots. While Cordelia and Agnes followed the main procession of students, Benji hung back to compare notes with his buddies about some new video game they had all been playing.

"So it turns out this place is haunted," Cordelia told Agnes. "Nothing scary. Just the dude who built it. I was thinking we could—"

Cordelia noticed—much to her annoyance—that Agnes was texting someone. "Don't worry. I'm listening," Agnes said. She added a smile, which was a far more common occurrence now that her braces had been removed.

"My Agnes! No sharing!" Cordelia whined, playfully reaching for the phone. "Who is this mysterious person who's more important than me?"

"Just this guy Mark. I met him at the college where I do that STEM program."

"I thought that was only for girls."

"It is. Mark's in a special physics program for the gifted and talented. He had a question about quantum mechanics."

"Was it 'What is quantum mechanics?'"

"A bit more complicated than that." Agnes rattled off one last text and slipped the phone in her pocket. "Done now. Sorry."

"I forgive you. But only if Mark has romantic potential. I'm picturing tall, big blue eyes, lab coat."

"Short, stocky, Patriots sweatshirt." Agnes's cheeks colored slightly. "As for romantic potential, he did lend me a pencil last week. And not just any old pencil. The fancy mechanical kind."

"What a flirt!"

"Speaking of romance . . ." Agnes whispered in a teasing tone, linking her arm through Cordelia's. "Benji and Vivi have been broken up for months now. And he was totally staring at you during social studies yesterday."

"You're crazy."

"I'm a scientist. My powers of observation are unparalleled."

"I probably had something on my face."

"Yeah. Your eyes and nose and mouth. And Benji couldn't get enough of them."

"Stop," Cordelia said, blushing. "Benji and Vivi barely talk these days."

"And this is a problem because . . . ?"

"They used to be really good friends before they dated. And now they're not."

"That's how it goes sometimes," Agnes said.

"Exactly! If Benji and I started dating, all we'd be doing is stamping an expiration date on our friendship. So many things have already changed. The dehaunter stole my job. Mr. Shadow went back home. Ezra moved. I can't risk losing Benji too!"

"Or, as an alternate take, we made the school safe for all the ghosts, Mr. Shadow and Dr. Roqueni are finally getting along again, Ezra's mom got an awesome new job, and if you and Benji dated, you'd be the cutest couple since Asuna and Kirito."

"I don't know who those people are."

"And speaking of change being a good thing," Agnes continued, "remember that girl who moved here from California and really hated her new school because it was full of ghosts, but now her entire life revolves around–"

"That reminds me! We're graduating from Shadow

School in a few months! More change!"

"I think you missed my point there."

They started up the wooden ramp that jutted from the hull of the ark. The view was breathtaking: mountain peaks, the morning sun, a forest of snow-dappled hemlocks. Cordelia glanced back at Benji, who was still talking to his friends. He must have sensed she was looking in his direction because he returned her gaze.

Cordelia quickly looked away.

They reached a scenic landing just outside the main entrance where visitors could pose for photographs. Mr. Derleth was standing next to a big blue storage bin on wheels.

"No bags permitted inside," he said, cupping his gloved hands to his mouth. "Leave them here. You can pick them up on your way back to the bus."

Cordelia put her head down and kept walking. *I saved you from being possessed by an evil gardener,* she thought, quickening her pace. *Just let the whole bag thing slide. . . .*

"Cordelia," Mr. Derleth said in a cheery voice.

"Oops," she said, turning around. "I didn't hear you. Sorry."

"Uh-huh. No need to lug that thing around." He gave her a knowing smile. "There's nothing in there you need today."

Cordelia could see what was happening. Dr. Roqueni had known she would bring the spectercles, despite telling her otherwise. Mr. Derleth was there to stop her. With a grunt of frustration, Cordelia tossed the bag in the bin. Someday she might see a ghost outside of Shadow School. But it wouldn't be today.

The students congregated in a massive entrance hall. Hats were removed, hair patted into place, gloves stuffed inside pockets. Coats, for the most part, stayed on. The temperature was warmer than outside, but not exactly toasty.

"Whoa," Agnes said. "This place is even cooler on the inside!"

Cordelia gazed up at the wooden ceiling high overhead, drinking in its cathedral vastness. There were winding ramps and hanging walkways everywhere. Looking along the length of the ark, Cordelia felt momentarily disoriented by its size, like standing on the edge of a skyscraper and gazing down at the sidewalk below. Beams of light pierced the dimly lit bowels, crossing in a series of giant X's that seemed to warn visitors to proceed no further.

Mr. Derleth and the parent chaperones corralled the students toward a presentation area in the center of the hall. Benji rejoined the girls, and the trio squished together on one of the semicircular benches set up for visitors.

While taking her seat, Agnes accidentally kicked over Mason James's water bottle. It made a loud clanging noise.

"Watch it!" Mason exclaimed, checking the bottle for damage. "This is a limited edition. It cost ninety dollars!"

Benji scoffed. "Who pays ninety bucks for a water bottle?"

"People who can," Mason said with a superior little smile. "I wouldn't expect *you* to understand. By the way, I saw your sister the other day. First year at Shadow School, right? Cute kid."

Cordelia felt Benji's body go rigid. "Watch it."

"Funny thing. I recognized the sweater she was wearing. My sister used to wear it all the time. We give all our old clothes to charity, so . . . I'm glad it's being put to good use."

"My family doesn't take charity," Benji said.

Mason's gaze lingered over Benji's ratty old hoodie. "Maybe you should start."

Perhaps things would have escalated—Benji had a temper, especially when his family was involved—but at that point an elderly woman walked to the front of the audience and cleared her throat. She was wearing a maroon jacket, a glittery butterfly pendant, and a button that said ARK ME A QGESTION!

"Thank you so much for coming today," the woman said. Her voice was clear and strong. "My name is Mrs. Russell, and you are in for a treat today—a real treat!"

Mason took a long slug from his water bottle. Cordelia patted Benji's arm. "He's not worth it."

Benji gave the briefest of nods and slouched in his seat.

"Gideon's Ark is not only an architectural marvel," Mrs. Russell continued. "It's one of the largest natural history museums in the world. But I'm getting ahead of myself." She took a step to the side, revealing a glass case exhibiting an antique toy ark. "Let's start with a small boy growing up in the farmlands of Illinois. A small boy with a small ark . . . and big dreams."

Over the next hour, Mrs. Russell related the history of Seamus Gideon in painstaking detail. As a child, he had been obsessed with the biblical story of Noah and the flood, so when Seamus became rich enough, he decided to build an ark of his own. His initial plan had been to fill it with living animals and create the world's first floating zoo, but when that proved impractical, Gideon decided to preserve animals that were already dead. Over the following two decades, he collected as many species as possible.

As Mrs. Russell droned on and on, Cordelia's attention began to wander. She twisted in her seat and saw two grown-ups standing behind the kids: a burly, bearded man who looked like he should be felling trees somewhere and a young woman with auburn hair. They made an odd pair. Cordelia assumed they were chaperones, though she didn't remember seeing them earlier.

"Mr. Gideon passed away one tragic morning in 1973," Mrs. Russell said, holding a hand to her butterfly pendant. "But his legacy lives on! Within these walls you will find over two thousand species of animals, all perfectly preserved by the finest taxidermists in America, many by Mr. Gideon himself. But since the wonders of the natural world are hardly enough to hold the attention of today's youth"—a pause here to deliver a withering glare at a student sneaking a peek at his phone—"we are also providing you with a scavenger hunt. There are twenty-six different species to find, from the silky anteater to the plains zebra. Good luck!"

The students rose from their seats, eager to stretch their legs, while Mr. Derleth and the chaperones passed out lists.

"I *love* scavenger hunts!" Agnes exclaimed. "My mom used to hide different fungus samples all over the house when I was little. I had to find them *and* identify them. Double the fun!"

"We need to have a long talk about your childhood," Cordelia said.

"Anything beats sitting in class," Benji said. "And the best part? No ghosts! This might be a school day, but it feels like a vacation to me."

Unlike Cordelia, Benji had always viewed his ability to see the ghosts as a burden, not a gift. It made her sad. She wished he loved the ghosts as much as she did. They had only been away from Shadow School for an hour, and Cordelia already missed them.

What am I going to do when I graduate? she thought.

They headed into the bowels of Gideon's Ark.

Scavenger Hunt

The walls of the third-floor landing were carved with relief sculptures of tropical birds. Dust motes danced in the sunlight that filtered in between the ceiling beams. Benji peered over the thick rope that protected visitors from a messy fall and whistled.

"Long way down," he said.

"I'll take your word for it," Agnes replied, refusing to look. She had no problem allowing tarantulas to climb up her arm or dissecting a squid's eye, but heights were a different story.

They crossed the landing and entered a wide, creaky corridor. It was darker in this part of the ark. Hearing the wind swirl outside, Cordelia could easily imagine that they were riding the ocean waves instead of sitting on top of a mountain.

Dozens of eyes watched them pass.

If the birds had been dangling from fishing lines or behind the glass windows of museum-style dioramas, Cordelia might have felt more at ease. But Gideon had wanted his ark to feel as authentic as possible, so the dead birds had been secured in dome-shaped cages, as though there was a possibility they might come to life and try to escape. Concealed speakers played chirping noises, adding to the eerie atmosphere.

"This guy clearly didn't have enough stuffed animals as a kid," Benji muttered.

"They're not stuffed," Agnes said as she gleefully flitted from exhibit to exhibit. Each species was represented by two birds—a male and a female—which somehow made things even creepier. "A good taxidermist doesn't need to open the body cavity at all. They just carefully remove and preserve the skin, then mount it onto an armature."

Benji stared at a white pelican, its long beak poised to snag a fish that would never come. "So, I'm not looking at a dead bird. I'm looking at a dead bird's skin stretched over some kind of . . . mannequin?"

"Exactly."

"You know that's not any better, right? It might actually be worse."

Agnes crossed her arms. "Taxidermy is a highly respected art that's been used to preserve animals for centuries."

"By serial killers?"

"By scientists!"

"And serial killers," Benji said, "and probably the occasional serial killer who was also a scientist."

As Agnes did her best to stomp on Benji's foot, Cordelia took a closer look at a pair of small birds with vibrant blue feathers. A placard below the cage read:

SPLENDID FAIRYWREN, AUSTRALIA

"Are those eyes real?" Cordelia asked.

Agnes shook her head. "Probably just glass. Eyes are a pain to preserve, so taxidermists either make their own or order from one of the specialized companies online. Some of the eyes are truly beautiful—like works of art!"

"Now I know what to get you for your birthday," Cordelia said.

Agnes was clearly pleased by the idea. "Just so you know, snowy owls have *gorgeous* eyes. They would look so cute on my desk!"

"Serial killer," Benji whispered.

The kids spotted one of the birds they needed for the scavenger hunt (cedar waxwings, New Hampshire) and checked it off their list. With this minor achievement under their belt, they followed the main corridor into dark, mazelike passageways that seemed to stretch forever. Occasionally they passed a group of fellow students using their phones to light their path—or just using their phones, period. They found Vivi and a cute boy named Austin Ferris laughing in front of the slender-snouted crocodile, but if Benji was bothered by this, Cordelia didn't notice.

She had other things on her mind.

Even though her initial plan with the spectercles had failed, she was keeping her eyes peeled for the ghost of Seamus Gideon. *Elijah Shadow could see them*, Cordelia thought, staring into the darkness and willing it to move. *Why not me?* The scavenger hunt allowed her to search for Seamus without being obvious about it, which was good. She was too embarrassed to tell her friends what she was really doing. Benji and Agnes knew all about her numerous attempts to see ghosts outside of Shadow School, and they might find her refusal to accept what had already been proven, time and time again, a little sad.

The morning dragged on. By the time they had reached the middle of their list (capybaras, South America), Cordelia was starting to give up and Benji was bored. Only Agnes retained her enthusiasm. Her ponytail bopped up and down as she zipped between exhibits, checking each placard for the next animal on their list. She grew tired of waiting for her sluggish friends and forged ahead without them.

Cordelia's stomach grumbled.

"Hungry?" Benji asked.

"You heard that?"

"My tío heard that. Not the one you met. The one who lives in Peru."

Cordelia smacked him on the arm. "It's not my fault. I'm starving."

"Me too. I won't lie. Some of these animals are starting to look pretty tasty."

"Eww."

"Come on, slowpokes!" Agnes called back. "That tomato frog's around here somewhere! I can feel it!"

"Is a tomato frog even real?" Benji asked.

"It's on the list," Cordelia said with a shrug. "Do you think it's called a tomato frog because it eats tomatoes or because it looks like a tomato?"

Benji laughed. "Beats me. But this place isn't so bad. At least we get to hang out."

Their eyes met, and Cordelia was suddenly aware that she could no longer hear Agnes—or anyone else, for that matter.

"So," Benji said, scratching the back of his head, "there's this new horror movie that just came out. It's about"—he made air quotes—"'ghosts.' You want to check it out? I figured we'd get a kick out of all the things they get spectacularly wrong."

"Fun! Agnes will have a field day. I'll bring my big pocketbook so we can sneak her brownies into the theater again."

"Actually," Benji said, suddenly unable to meet her eyes. "I was thinking that Ag could sit this one out. Like, it could just be us. Is that okay?"

He's asking me out, Cordelia thought in astonishment. She didn't know what to say. Images flashed through her head like a montage in a cheesy movie: sharing popcorn, inching closer together during the scary parts, holding hands in the hallway at school, the jealous whispers of the popular girls.

The word *yes* hovered close to her lips.

But was she ready to go on a first date? It was a watershed moment, the gate between *before* and *after*, a sign that high school was on the horizon and her years at Shadow School were drawing to a close.

"I don't think so," Cordelia said. "I'm sorry."

She could tell she had hurt Benji's feelings. "That's cool," he said, jamming his hands into his pockets. "It's probably a stupid movie anyway. Besides, I shouldn't be wasting money right now."

Cordelia grasped onto this potential segue, eager to change the subject. "Your dad have any luck finding a new job yet?"

"He's been interviewing left and right, but there's not much out there. Everyone's hurting. My mom's hours just got cut at the restaurant, so now she's freaking out more than ever. I've been bagging groceries and shoveling snow to try and help out, but that's just—"

Benji noticed something behind Cordelia and lowered his voice. "Let's keep moving. I don't need this guy hearing my life story."

They started to walk. Cordelia checked over her shoulder, trying to catch a glimpse of their eavesdropper. All she saw was a pair of panthers whose green eyes seemed to glow in the dim light.

"What guy?" she asked.

"Behind us."

Cordelia looked again. Longer this time. "There's no one there."

"How are you missing him? He's right there!"

There was no one behind them that Cordelia could see—which left only one possibility. "Does he have long white hair?" she asked. "And glasses that look too big for his face?"

"That's him!"

"Oh no. Benji—you're not going to like this."

"What?"

"I saw an old photo of Seamus Gideon downstairs. It was taken just before he died."

"No."

"He had long white hair."

"No!"

"And glasses too big for his face. It's a ghost, Benji. I can't see him. But you can."

"You're wrong!" Benji exclaimed. The desperation in his voice nearly broke her heart. "It's just a normal, *living* old man. I'll prove it."

He turned around and waved to what appeared to be an empty corridor. "Excuse me, sir," he said, craning his neck to look up at someone taller than himself. "Do you know the way back to the main floor?"

Cordelia strained to see something. A blur. A wavering. Anything. But as far as she could tell, Benji was talking to the air. She felt an unwelcome pang of jealousy. *It's not fair. He doesn't even like the ghosts.*

The smile faded from Benji's lips.

"No worries," he said, backing away. "We'll figure it out."

He rejoined Cordelia and gripped her arm. "Move," he whispered, guiding her away at a pace just short of a run.

"What's wrong?"

"It's a ghost. You were right about that. But different from the ones at school. I didn't like the way he was looking at me. His eyes . . ."

Benji clenched her arm tighter. His pace quickened.

"What about his eyes?" Cordelia asked.

"They're made of glass."

They retraced their steps in the direction of the main hall. The dead man kept pace. Benji and Cordelia thought about running, then decided against it. Ghosts could float and vanish and pass through walls. If Seamus wanted to catch up to them, he would. No need to dare him to do it.

When Cordelia was younger, she had been afraid of ghosts, just as she had been afraid of the monster that scratched at her closet door each night. Really, though, she was frightened of the same thing everyone fears: the unknown. Being able to see the ghosts had rendered that fear powerless. What you could see, you could know. What you could see, you could hide from.

Her fear of ghosts had been rekindled.

Cordelia asked, "Why is he following us?"

"Because I can see him, I think," Benji said, doing

another check over his shoulder. "You know how some ghosts are funny about that."

"So stop looking!"

"It's a little late for that."

Cordelia's phone dinged. It was a text from Agnes, who had gone downstairs to join the rest of the students for lunch. Everyone was wondering where they were. Texting as fast as she could, Cordelia tried to give a rundown of the situation: gideon ghost behind us, benji can see, i can't. BENJI ASKED ME OUT!!! realize not important right now but still

"We have to find the stairs," Cordelia said. She thought the ghost might leave them alone once they joined a large group. In general, the dead shied away from crowds.

Benji sighed with relief. "Actually, I think we're okay. He stopped following us. He's just, like, closing his eyes. And . . . um . . . raising his hands into the air."

"Maybe we should walk a little faster."

Something rattled to her left. Cordelia turned and saw two spider monkeys rocking their fake cage back and forth, trying to escape. She struggled to make sense of this new brand of weirdness. The spider monkeys were dead. Less than dead, really—just skin mounted over a frame.

"You can see this, right?" Benji asked.

"See—yes," Cordelia said. "Believe? No."

The monkeys' movements were jerky and stiff. They might have looked like full-fledged animals, but they lacked the complicated system of bones, muscles, and sinew needed to move smoothly; their bodies were meant for display, not life. One of them strained too hard to lift the cage and a glass eye popped out and rolled across the floor. At the same time, Cordelia heard a *BANGBANGBANG* and spun around to find a pair of warthogs headbutting the wall of their wooden pen. The larger one butted too hard and its curved horn snapped off. The wound leaked clay and iron mesh.

Cordelia and Benji ran toward the exit. Real-world sounds of escape—rattling, snapping, crashing—drowned out the jungle noises playing over the speaker. There was movement everywhere: a furry rodent skittering beneath their feet, chimpanzees swinging from the rafters, giraffes lurching their long necks over the walls of their pen. Cordelia stopped for a moment to catch her breath, and a leathery wing brushed her ear.

A few minutes later, they reached the second-floor landing. Cordelia leaned over the railing and saw that things were far worse than she had imagined.

4

The Two Worlds

The large hall beneath them was overrun with animals, as though there had been an escape at the world's most horrifying zoo. Fortunately, the taxidermic creatures were too slow and awkward to be effective hunters. Most students were able to elude them and sprint to the exit, where Mr. Derleth waved them to safety.

"Gideon's right there," Benji said, pointing to the center of the chaos. "How is he doing this?"

"He's not a normal ghost. He's a phantom."

They had come across Gideon's kind before. Ghosts who had stuck around for so long that their jealousy for the living had infected them with special powers, such as the ability to move objects with their mind or possess the living. Often they looked different as well, more like monsters than the humans they used to be.

"We've never met a phantom that can bring dead animals back to life," Benji said.

"It's a field trip," Cordelia said. "We're supposed to learn new things." A pair of bushy-tailed squirrels darted down the railing of the ramp, teeth flashing; Cordelia swatted them over the side. "How do we stop him?"

"We don't," Benji said. "We just leave. He can't follow us. Once we get out of this ark, we're home free."

"There's still a few kids down there. We can't just abandon them. We're the only ones who can—*you're* the only one who can see the ghost."

Benji gave a reluctant nod. Most students had already escaped, but not all. A few kids were trapped in the gift shop, a polar bear pawing at the glass door. Others hunkered down behind trash bins or benches, afraid to risk coming out into the open.

There was no sign of Agnes.

"This is probably a long shot," Benji said as they hustled down the ramp. "But any idea what Gideon's Brightkey might be?"

"Easy. It's the toy ark that lady showed us—the one Gideon loved so much when he was a kid. But it won't work. Brights are just a Shadow School thing, remember? That's why Elijah had to create those model houses to trap ghosts out in the wild."

"It might distract him, at least. Give you a chance to get everyone out of here."

"Worth a shot," Cordelia said.

They split up at the bottom of the ramp: Benji to grab the ark, Cordelia to usher the remaining students to safety. Most of the kids were frozen in place, too scared to move, so she had to guide them to the ramp—pushing, kicking, or dodging past one animal or another. Outside of minor scrapes, no one seemed hurt.

Cordelia kept an eye out for Agnes, but she was nowhere to be found—which was worrisome. Agnes would never abandon them. Something must have happened.

"Cordelia!" Benji exclaimed.

He was standing on a long display case entitled THE MIRACLE OF TAXIDERMY. A dozen animals milled beneath him. Of particular concern was a gargantuan gorilla attempting to scale the display with its one remaining arm.

"I got the ark," Benji said, leaning over the side to show her. "But then I made the mistake of looking right at Gideon again. He really doesn't like that. All the animals started chasing me."

A baby rhino thrust its head upward in an attempt to impale Benji with its horn. He danced away just in time.

"I'll give it to Gideon," Cordelia said.

Benji tossed the toy high in the air and she caught it with two hands. Cordelia doubted the little ark would send Gideon into his Bright, but she could at least give it to him and see what happened. It wasn't like they had any other ideas.

One problem. She couldn't see the ghost.

"You have to guide me," Cordelia said. When Benji didn't respond, she saw he had bigger concerns: the gorilla had succeeded in pulling itself atop the case and was closing the distance between them, the knuckles of its single hand grazing the wood.

Benji leaped from the display and took off. A dozen animals licked his heels.

Cordelia was on her own.

"Gideon?" she asked, blindly offering the ark in various directions. "This belongs to you. Don't you want it?"

Something slid into her foot. Cordelia turned with the ark held high over her head, ready to pummel the snarling goat or spitting llama or whatever else was attacking her.

It wasn't an animal. It was her bookbag.

"Mr. Derleth thought you might need that!" Agnes

exclaimed. She had just reentered the ark through the main entrance and looked out of breath, as though she had run the entire way.

"Thanks," Cordelia said, relieved to see that her friend was okay.

She dumped her bag and let the contents clatter to the floor: phone, thermos, sketchbook, pencil case, tube of half-melted lip balm, and three pairs of spectercles (though Benji, she now knew, would never require their assistance). Cordelia tossed the case with the platypus sticker to Agnes, who was standing over her now, and opened the next one.

It was empty.

"Where are the spectercles?" Cordelia asked.

"They're there—just invisible," Agnes said. "We're not in Shadow School, remember? Your Sight doesn't work here."

"How could I forget?" Cordelia asked, feeling inside the case. There was something smooth and cold in there. Lenses. She slipped her fingers beneath them and felt a band in the back, as thin and rubbery as a jellyfish tentacle.

Cordelia closed her eyes and pulled the spectercles over her head.

They seemed to tighten on their own, and she shuddered as a sudden idea occurred to her. They had no idea how the spectercles worked, or where they had been made. What if she was looking through the eyes of a creature capable of seeing the ghosts? A creature that might—in some way, shape, or form—still be alive?

It doesn't matter, she thought, *as long as they work.*

Cordelia opened her eyes.

Two worlds spun around her. The first, moving clockwise, was the world she knew. Walls, floor, lights. Reality. The second world turned in the opposite direction. It danced with smoky shadows and colors she had never seen before.

Cordelia started to fall. A steadying hand grasped her arm.

"Give it a second," Agnes said. "It'll pass."

The twin worlds slowed, like opposing carousels nearing the ends of their rides, and finally merged. The ark was still once more. Cordelia blinked her teary eyes. She could now see that Agnes was wearing her spectercles. They were dark with concave lenses, like goggles intended to shield a swimmer from the glare of bioluminescent fish.

"Do you see the ghost?" Agnes asked.

Cordelia examined the hall and spotted a tall man wearing a vest and bow tie. Seamus Gideon. His appearance was blurred, like a photo taken out of focus.

"He's right there!" Cordelia exclaimed, thrilled that

her Sight was working again.

"Where?" Agnes asked.

"There!" Cordelia said, jabbing her finger in the ghost's direction. "Can't you see him?"

"No!" Agnes sighed with frustration and yanked off her spectercles. "These are useless here!"

"But mine work. How can that be?"

"We'll figure it out later. Benji needs our help!"

Agnes was right. Benji was in his element, sprinting and juking as though he was playing the most important soccer match of his life, but he was also looking a little winded. Cordelia knew he couldn't keep dodging the animals for much longer.

"Hey!" she screamed. "Over here!"

Gideon regarded her with glass eyes that bulged from their sockets like oversized marbles. His lips curled into a snarl. *Benji was right*, Cordelia thought. *He doesn't like it when you look at him.* A three-legged snow leopard abandoned its pursuit of Benji and took a few jerky strides in her direction.

Cordelia laid the ark at Gideon's feet. The phantom dismissed it with a glance.

"What's happening?" Agnes asked. "Did he go into his Bright yet?"

"Not exactly."

Gideon pointed at Cordelia, and all the animals

swiveled their heads in her direction. They started toward the kids, slowly and steadily, closing their ranks to cut off any possible escape route.

Benji rejoined his friends. He was out of breath and had collected a few rips in his pants and a long scratch on his cheek. "Anyone have any ideas?" he asked.

"Puppy Snuggling Centers," Agnes offered. "You pay an hourly fee, and you can snuggle with all the puppies you want."

"Ideas about our *current situation*," Benji clarified.

"I got nothing," Agnes said.

The taxidermied animals drew closer, their movements as jerky as zombies. One goat had nearly lost its head. It dangled by a few strands of black thread and watched them with yellow, upside-down eyes.

"Don't worry, kids," said an unfamiliar voice. "We got this."

The speaker was the young woman Cordelia had seen earlier. She was standing just beyond the circle of animals with the burly man by her side. He held a long duffel bag in one hand.

"Where's the ghost?" the woman asked.

Cordelia and Benji, too dumbfounded to speak, simply pointed. The man swung his duffel bag and cleared a path through the animals, allowing his partner to slip inside the circle and unsheathe a long rod from behind her back. At first, Cordelia thought it was some type of weapon, but then the woman pressed a button and a telescopic rod shot out like an umbrella and unfolded into a flat screen.

"Here," she said, handing the device to Benji. The entire contraption, now complete, looked like a TV on a stick. "Make sure this is turned in Gideon's direction. He needs to see."

She tapped her watch and a series of short videos jumped to life on the screen. Bacon sizzling in a frying pan. Children kicking a ball in the street. Ocean waves crashing across a beach. The images were crisp and clear, the sound sharp. Gideon was mesmerized. One by one, the animals toppled over. Their master was too distracted to keep them alive.

"Keep it still," the woman told Benji. The man joined them and withdrew three black poles from his duffel bag. With practiced ease, he extended the first one to well over six feet and placed its base on the floor near Gideon. The phantom's attention remained riveted to the screen, where a newborn baby was crying.

"What's with the movies?" Agnes asked. She couldn't see the ghost's reaction, so they must have seemed particularly strange.

"They're distracting Gideon," Cordelia said. "He can't stop watching them."

"Why?" Agnes asked.

"Because it's life," the woman said. "Sounds. Sights. Sensations. Everything ghosts miss the most. Everything they crave in death."

On the screen, a woman took a sip of coffee.

"Who are you?" Cordelia asked.

"My name's Laurel. That's Kyle. He's not much of a talker. We got a call last night saying there had been some unusual activity here and we should come check it out first thing in the morning. Good thing we did." She took a moment to examine each of the kids. "Can you all see the ghosts?"

Cordelia hesitated before responding. Dr. Roqueni had trained them to hide their Sight from others. But after what these two had witnessed, was there any point denying it?

"Benji and I can see them," Cordelia said, self-consciously touching the spectercles. "My name's Cordelia. That's Agnes. She can't see the ghosts, but she can do lots of other things."

"Pleased to meet you," said Laurel.

Kyle finished extending the second rod and leaned it against the first one. The two ends snapped together with a magnetic *click*.

"What's he doing?" Agnes asked.

Laurel lifted a sleek machine the size of a car battery

from the duffel bag and gently placed it on the floor. "Building an SCU," she replied. "Spectral Containment Unit. Kyle calls it a ghost tent, but I think that sounds silly."

Kyle snapped the third rod into place while Laurel removed a brass tube from a carrying case on her belt. She pushed the open end of the tube onto a nozzle at the top of the machine, securing the connection with two iron clamps.

"We good?" she asked Kyle. He finished connecting a wire to the pyramid's vertex and gave her a thumbs-up. Laurel flicked a few switches on the machine and a loud humming noise reverberated throughout the hall. Indigo bolts of lightning snapped between the rods. Cordelia saw flashes of light reflected in Gideon's glass eyes.

And then he vanished.

"Whoa!" Benji exclaimed.

"Where'd he go?" Cordelia asked.

"Right there," Laurel said, pointing to the top of the machine.

Cordelia fell to her knees for a closer look. Through a tiny window in the brass tube, she saw swirling blue mist that hadn't been there before.

"That's *Gideon*?" Cordelia asked.

Laurel nodded. "Cool, right?"

"Is he okay?"

"Totally. We just made his spirit a little more travel-sized."

Laurel checked an indicator, which *dinged* pleasantly as it flashed from red to green, and removed the clamps holding the tube in place. With one smooth motion, she yanked the tube off the nozzle; a new rubber cork had been inserted, presumably to keep the ghost inside. Laurel deftly slipped the tube back into its padded case and buckled it shut. Meanwhile, Kyle disassembled the ghost tent and returned the pieces to the duffel bag.

"I have so many questions," Cordelia said. "I don't even know where to start."

Laurel smiled. "Another time. Kyle and I need to go. Drop me a line and we'll chat about your future."

She handed Cordelia a cream-colored business card. Above a handwritten phone number were two words printed in a stylish font:

SHADY REST

"What's Shady Rest?" Cordelia asked, but Laurel and Kyle were already headed out the door.

5

Dr. Roqueni's Announcement

The moment school ended, Cordelia, Benji, and Agnes headed straight to the basement. Elijah Shadow's office lay beneath a hidden trapdoor. Shelves packed with leather-bound volumes lined the walls, and a drafting table sat in the center of the room, surrounded by long cabinets stuffed with blueprints. The air was as musty as a seaside library. Cordelia had tried adding a few different species of plants to liven things up, but they never survived for long.

In the corner where Elijah's bones had lain for nearly a century (before being properly interred this summer), Darius Shadow was chatting with Mr. Derleth.

The old man saw them and chuckled.

"There they are," he said. "You kids can't even go on a boring old field trip without stirring up trouble! So now you can see ghosts outside of Shadow School too?"

"Benji can," Cordelia said, managing a weak smile. "I need to use the spectercles."

"So what? I wear glasses when I sit down with the newspaper each morning. Doesn't mean I can't read." He scratched the gray stubble on his chin. "I'm sorely tempted to pop into a few haunted houses and give my own spectercles a go. See what I can see."

"Sorry, Mr. Shadow," Agnes said. "Mine didn't work today, so I'm fairly certain that will be the case for yours as well. I have a theory—"

Mr. Shadow grinned. "Of course you do."

"—that the spectercles are like magnifying glasses. They can augment someone's preexisting ability to see the ghosts. But if there's no Sight to begin with, they're not going to do you any good."

Cordelia said, "But if that were the case, they wouldn't work in Shadow School, either."

"Shadow School's special. Maybe the archimancy is so powerful that it gives everyone a little Sight to work with." She noticed Cordelia's dismayed reaction and quickly added, "But you're the real thing! Otherwise your spectercles wouldn't have worked outside the school at all! Your Sight is just . . . you know . . ."

"Weak," Cordelia said.

She noticed that Benji had moved away from the others. He had barely spoken since their return.

"I see Benji isn't too keen on this latest development," Mr. Shadow said. "I'm not surprised. That boy's a good egg, but he's never embraced his gift. He reminds me of Aria in that way."

"He'll come around. I'll talk to him."

"Leave him be, Cordelia. He's got his way of thinking; you've got yours. Don't make the same mistake I made by trying to change him."

Mr. Shadow was referring to his niece, Dr. Roqueni. He had forced her to spend day after day among the spirits of Shadow School when she was little, even though she wanted nothing to do with them. Eventually, she came to hate him for it. Mr. Shadow was trying to make amends for these earlier misdeeds, but Dr. Roqueni hadn't completely forgiven him. Cordelia hoped it wasn't too late.

The trapdoor opened and Dr. Roqueni entered the office.

"Sorry I'm late," she said, taking a seat at the drafting table. "I had to finish writing an email to the parents about today's incident."

"That's a tough one," Mr. Derleth said. "How'd you spin it?"

Dr. Roqueni read from her phone.

"'It has come to my attention that during today's field trip to a local landmark, some eighth graders claim to have been attacked by animals that magically came to life. Obviously, this is not true. After an in-depth investigation, the school has come to the conclusion that this incident was some kind of elaborate student prank.'"

The kids burst into laughter.

"Glad I could provide you with some amusement after such a trying experience," Dr. Roqueni said.

"Sorry," Cordelia said, "but is anyone actually going to believe that?"

"The kids won't. But I've found that adults will latch on to any explanation, however unlikely, as long as the world can continue to turn in the same predictable fashion they know and understand." She slipped the phone back into her pocket. "I never should have sent you there in the first place. I knew the ark was haunted. What was I thinking?"

"Gideon's ghost was supposed to be nice," Cordelia said in a consoling voice. "The website says he once guided a lost child back to her parents."

"He wasn't so nice today," muttered Benji.

"It's not his fault he turned into a phantom. And no one actually got hurt, so he wasn't *that* bad—"

"Cordelia," Benji said, clamping his head between

his hands. "Today is not the day for your 'all ghosts are precious and wonderful' routine."

"I understand how you must be feeling—"

Benji scoffed. "You're literally the last person on earth who could possibly understand how I'm feeling right now. You probably think I'm lucky I can see the ghosts. Don't you?"

"It's a gift."

"I wish that were true. If it were a gift, I could return it. But I can't. I'm stuck seeing ghosts everywhere I go for the rest of my life."

He flicked his hoodie over his head and slunk out of the room. As the trapdoor settled back into place, Dr. Roqueni shared a long look with Mr. Derleth. "That poor boy. Are you sure he'll be okay while I'm gone?"

"I'll keep an eye on him," Mr. Derleth said.

"'While I'm gone'?" Cordelia asked. "What's that mean?"

Dr. Roqueni fiddled with her glasses. When she finally spoke, her voice was soft and uncertain. "I'm taking a leave of absence. Last year was . . . difficult. I need some time. I've been the principal here for nearly twenty years, without a vacation. Now that the dehaunter is up and running, it seems like the perfect opportunity."

"But you can't just leave," Cordelia said. "You're the

principal. Who's going to run the school?"

Mr. Derleth raised his hand. "I have an adminis-trator's license. We should be able to survive for a few months." He swallowed nervously and looked at Dr. Roqueni. "But no longer than that. You seriously have to come back."

"Where are you going?" Agnes asked.

"Uncle Darius has graciously arranged a trip to Europe. It's always been a dream of mine. Visiting the most famous museums in the world. Drinking espresso in outdoor cafés. Seeing Paris from the top of the Eiffel Tower."

There was a giddiness in the principal's voice that Cordelia had never heard before. It made her seem younger.

"I'm sorry you had to wait so long," Mr. Shadow said, "but better late than never."

"You're still joining me in Italy, right?"

"I wouldn't miss it for the world."

It had been a strange day. First a phantom, now a European vacation. Cordelia was surprised but happy. Dr. Roqueni definitely needed the break, and it seemed like this might make her and Mr. Shadow a family again.

"I'll miss you," Cordelia said. "Both of you. But you're going to have the best time ever."

"I'll miss you all as well," said Dr. Roqueni. "I'm afraid I've sidetracked our very important conversation. I've heard bits and pieces from Mr. Derleth, but tell me what happened today in your own words. Don't leave out a single detail. I'm especially interested in these two strangers who appeared out of nowhere. They don't know you can see ghosts, right?"

Cordelia heard the fear in her voice and knew she would have to lie. "No way. We never even talked to them."

Agnes flinched a tiny bit but played along. Cordelia would explain later: If Dr. Roqueni thought the kids were in the slightest danger, she would never go on her trip. For that reason, Cordelia told a slightly revised version of events, leaving out the part where the kids helped Laurel and Kyle or had any sort of interaction with them whatsoever. The adults listened carefully, asking the occasional question.

"You were smart to stay out of sight," Dr. Roqueni said. "It's a relief that they captured the ghost and no one got hurt. But something about this feels off."

"I agree," Mr. Shadow added. "All that fancy equipment means deep pockets. I don't like that. If they're somehow making money from their dealings with the ghosts, it gives them a motive for wanting someone with your gifts. A bad motive. People don't say 'money is the root of all evil' just because it's catchy."

Dr. Roqueni gave her uncle an appreciative look for backing her up. Cordelia thought they were both being paranoid. Laurel and Kyle were obviously the good guys; they had helped save the students from an angry phantom!

"It doesn't matter," Cordelia said, trying to sound as blasé as possible. "We'll never see them again."

She thought that would put any reservations to rest, but judging from the suspicious looks the adults exchanged, she had grievously misplayed her hand.

"These people seem to know even more about the ghosts than we do, and you don't have the slightest desire to find out who they are?" Dr. Roqueni asked. "That's very unlike you, Cordelia. You're not going to do something foolish like try to contact them while I'm gone, are you?"

"No," Cordelia said, doing her best to recover. "Of course not. I would never—I mean, I *am* curious. Duh! It's me, right? But I already tried to track them down online and got *nowhere*. Whoever these people are, they're determined to remain a secret."

This, at least, had one foot in the realm of truth. Cordelia had googled "Shady Rest" on the long bus ride back to school and tried to narrow her search with terms like "ghost" and "New Hampshire." She had found a number of graveyards, and one hammock store, but nothing that related to Laurel and Kyle.

Good thing she had their phone number.

"You're positive they don't know you can see the ghosts?" Dr. Roqueni asked. "Maybe I should delay my trip just a few weeks. . . ."

"We're *fine*," Cordelia said. "Nothing dangerous is going to happen while you're gone. Promise."

6

Two Phone Calls and Some Texts

Cordelia waited until she was alone in her room that night before calling the number on the business card. The phone rang only once before someone answered.

"Hey there."

Cordelia instantly recognized Laurel's voice. She sounded like a rock singer whose throat was scratchy from a recent set.

"Hi. It's Cordelia. We met today at the ark."

She heard the squeaking of a rolling chair on the other end of the line and pictured Laurel leaning back, maybe putting her feet up on a desk. "Cordelia. I'm glad you called. That was something today. You handled yourself like a pro."

Cordelia's chest swelled up with pride. Unlike more traditional extracurricular activities, rescuing ghosts had never led to applause or trophies. It was nice to have her skills recognized. "Thanks. You were really awesome. With the ghost tent and movies and all that."

"It's what I do. But this can't be your first experience with ghosts. Give me some backstory. I don't even know your last name."

"Liu."

"Cordelia Liu. I like it. Tell me some things."

She didn't know where to begin. Archimancy? Brightkeys? Ghost scavengers? There was something effortlessly cool about Laurel—like the big sister Cordelia had always wanted—and she felt an intense desire to impress her. But talking about Shadow School would shine a light on conversational paths she wanted to keep dark. It was bad enough that she was disobeying Dr. Roqueni by calling Laurel in the first place. Giving away the Shadow family secrets would be a different sort of betrayal altogether.

"I've seen ghosts before," Cordelia said.

"Where?"

"Here and there."

Laurel waited for Cordelia to continue. She didn't.

"I get it," Laurel said. "I'm a stranger. Why would you trust me? I'd be the same way. I hope to earn your trust in time, Cordelia, but I know it's a two-way street. So why don't you ask your questions first? I'm sure you have a ton of them after what happened today."

"What's Shady Rest?"

"It's a company dedicated to saving ghosts."

"How?"

"By moving them to safer locations."

"Safer for who? The ghosts or the living?"

"Both."

Cordelia asked, "What does that mean, 'safer locations'?"

"New houses where they won't be disturbed. Or disturb others."

"How many ghosts have you moved?"

"Forty-three."

The number staggered Cordelia for a moment. "Whoa. Regular ghosts? Or special ghosts like Gideon?"

The squeaking chair again—perhaps Laurel sitting up this time. "So you know there's a difference?"

Cordelia winced. "Now I do. Gideon was different from the other ghosts I've seen. They were kind of chill."

"I see. Well, there's nothing to worry about. Most of

the ghosts we deal with at Shady Rest are completely harmless. The special ones like Gideon—we call those phantoms in our biz—are very, very rare."

We call them phantoms too, Cordelia thought. She asked, "Is the company just you and Kyle? Or are there others?"

"Kyle and I are the only ones who go out in the field, but there're quite a few people who work at Shady Rest."

"What do they do?"

Laurel sighed in a way that made Cordelia feel like an annoying little kid who had asked too many questions. "This is so hard to explain over the phone. It would be much easier to show you in person. You and your friends—what are their names again?"

"Benji and Agnes."

"All three of you should come to the village on Saturday. I'll give you a complete tour."

"Maybe," Cordelia said. This was all happening faster than she'd expected. "I have to talk to my friends first."

"You do? I'm a little surprised. You have such a rare gift, and I thought for sure you'd want to use it to help those who can no longer help themselves—"

I do, Cordelia thought. *More than anything.*

"—but maybe I read you wrong. Maybe you're okay

with letting your gift waste away, unused."

Cordelia clenched the phone, terrified that if she hung up, she'd never get another opportunity like this again. "I'll be there. I can't speak for my friends, though. I'm pretty sure Agnes will come, as long as you let her press a few buttons. I'm not so sure about Benji. This isn't really his thing."

"I saw the way he looks at you, Cordelia. I'm sure you can talk him into it."

They spent a few more minutes ironing out the details. When the call ended, Cordelia texted Agnes and gave her a full report. Her friend was excited to visit, but she had two concerns. First: How were they going to convince their parents to drive to a random "village" thirty minutes away and leave them there? Fortunately, Cordelia didn't think this was going to be a problem. Laurel had already concocted a cover story, and it sounded fairly plausible.

Agnes's second concern was one Cordelia shared as well: They had promised Dr. Roqueni they wouldn't contact Shady Rest, and now they were going behind her back. Cordelia assured Agnes—and, to a certain degree, herself—that they were keeping this a secret for the sake of Dr. Roqueni. After all, if they told her the truth, her once-in-a-lifetime trip would be ruined! The logic of this sounded reasonable in Cordelia's head, but more like a lame rationale when she said it out loud.

In either case, it worked. Agnes agreed to come.

Next up was Benji.

Cordelia knew he would be far harder—maybe even impossible—to convince, so she decided to call instead of text. It took him a long time to pick up the phone.

"Hey," he said. "Give me a sec."

She could barely hear him over the background noise. A TV was blasting, Sofia was practicing her trumpet, and Benji's two younger sisters were arguing in Spanish. Cordelia heard a door close and the sounds grew muffled. Benji had stepped into one of the bedrooms for a little privacy.

"I can't talk long. I still have to make dinner and help Eva with her homework."

Benji was always watching his three sisters. His parents found work when they could get it, which sometimes kept them out at odd hours. Although Mr. and Mrs. Núñez would have loved to hire a babysitter, they simply didn't have enough money. It had to be Benji.

Besides, he was good at it. His sisters adored him, and he was a great cook.

Thinking about the demands placed on her friend always made Cordelia feel spoiled and lazy. She was an only child whose only chore was taking out the trash, which she often forgot to do.

"I'll be fast," Cordelia said. "I talked to Laurel."

Benji's tone instantly became guarded. "Okay."

Cordelia filled him in on their conversation. Benji had to leave once to settle some sort of conflict involving an iPad, but other than that she had his complete attention. When she was done, he said, "I understand why you and Agnes want to check it out. But I'm going to pass."

"Laurel asked for you specifically."

"Good for Laurel. I'm not interested."

"Aren't you curious?"

Benji hesitated. "This is your thing, not mine."

"You can see them, Benji. It's your thing whether you like it or not. This feels like it could be something really cool. Laurel wants you—"

"I don't care what Laurel wants!"

"Fine. I want you to be there! Do you care about that?"

Silence on the other end.

"When?" Benji asked.

"Ten. I'm pretty sure my dad can drive us."

"I have to be back at two to babysit."

"No problem. You won't regret this, Benji. I think—"

There was a loud *thunk* in the other room, like something falling off a shelf, followed by a scream of "Sofia!"

Benji said, "I have to go."

"I'm sorry about today."

"It's not your fault I can see the ghosts."

"That's not what I meant. The other thing. When you asked me . . . what you asked me. And I said no."

One of his sisters started to cry. Maybe two. It was hard to tell.

"I really have to go," Benji said. "I'll see you tomorrow, okay?"

"Bye, Benji."

Cordelia held the phone in her hand and leaned back in her seat. She wondered if Benji had only agreed to go because he liked her. The possibility made her feel guilty, like she had tricked him into it. Did being the object of someone's affection convey a kind of responsibility? It was a new and confusing concept. She considered calling him back but decided against it. Benji had his hands full with his sisters. If she still felt guilty tomorrow, she could talk to him in school.

Cordelia spent the rest of the evening mining the internet for any additional information about Shady Rest. She found nothing.

Shady Rest

By the time Cordelia woke up that Saturday, her dad had already returned from Ludlow Bakery with a half dozen of their fabled bear claws. The box was still warm.

"Just in case your friends haven't had breakfast yet," he said.

"You didn't have to do that," said Cordelia, who already felt guilty enough for lying to him in the first place.

"You deserve it. I think it's great you three are giving up your entire Saturday to volunteer like this."

"It's really no big deal."

"Are you kidding? Most of these spoiled kids won't

wake up until lunchtime, and then it's nothing but their phone all day. But not my daughter! She's working her tail off to help others. Do you know how proud that makes Mom and me?"

"Thanks, Baba," Cordelia said, kissing him on the cheek. She took the box from his hands. "We should get going."

She wished she could tell her parents about the ghosts. They might not believe her. They might be proud of all the good she had done. Or they might sue the school and ground her until she was eighty-five. But at least she'd be done lying to them. They deserved better.

After graduation, Cordelia thought, *we'll sit down and have a really long talk.*

It was a morning made for hiding beneath blankets and adding extra logs to the fire. During the drive to Agnes's house, the car shuddered at every stop sign and even stalled out once. Mr. Liu grumbled into his tea.

Agnes was watching for them out the front window. She skipped to the car, all smiles. "Hey, Mr. Liu!"

"Good morning," Mr. Liu replied with a smile of his own. He was very fond of Agnes, who was his go-to for help whenever one of his Sudoku puzzles proved too challenging. "How are you?"

"Are those bear claws in that box? Because if so, I'm about to be spectacular!"

"Dig in."

"In a sec," Agnes said. As Mr. Liu backed out of the driveway, she bent her head over her phone and texted someone.

"Is that the mysterious Mark?" Cordelia whispered, just softly enough that her father couldn't hear her. She and Agnes had perfected this sort of pinpoint volume control over the course of numerous car rides.

"It's not Mark," Agnes said. "It's Kedar."

"Who's Kedar?"

"Mark's friend. He's in the science program too."

"Does he have a question about quantum mechanics?" Cordelia asked, trying to peek at the phone.

"Nah. We're just chatting."

"Uh-huh," Cordelia said.

Agnes slipped the phone into her pocket and grabbed a bear claw, taking a napkin to make sure she didn't get any crumbs on the floor.

"I can't believe Benji's actually coming," Cordelia said.

"He's trying to impress you. Let's face it, Cord. Fastest way to your heart? Do something ghosty."

"I just want to be friends."

"Ha!" Agnes said, wiping a crumb from her mouth. "You've had a crush on Benji since day one. It's inevitable that you'll get together. You're just being stubborn about it for some weird reason. Are you jealous because he can see the ghosts and you can't?"

"A little. But that's not it. I don't want things to change. The last three years have been perfect."

"Except for all the times we almost died."

"Except for that. And math."

They picked up Benji, who gave Mr. Liu a fist bump upon seeing the bear claws and downed one in five massive bites. He was starting on his second when Mr. Liu pulled onto the highway going south and drove toward Massachusetts, passing through a couple of nondescript towns before making a turn onto a private road. After crossing a wooden bridge too narrow for more than one car to pass at a time, they slowed before a white guardhouse with an attached boom gate that blocked further progress. A cheery sign announced that this was the entrance to Shady Rest: A Retirement Village.

A man wearing a tan uniform exited the guardhouse and approached their car. There was an iPad in his hands, giving Cordelia the impression that no one was allowed to enter without being on some sort of list. He saw the kids in the back seat and gave Mr. Liu a smile.

"These must be our volunteers," he said. "Thanks so much for coming. The residents are going to be so happy to meet you."

The guard pressed a button that lifted the gate, and they drove into the village. The first house they saw was a simple Craftsman bearing a Main Office sign. Mr. Liu pulled in front of it. Cordelia kissed her dad good-bye and said they would text him when they were done.

"Have fun hanging out with those old-timers," he said. "I'm sure you're going to hear some great stories."

As her father drove away, Cordelia looked deeper into the village. She could only see a few houses from where she was, but they were in excellent condition: a brown ranch with a rocking chair in the front yard, a rustic log cabin surrounded by evergreens, and a humble split-level that could have been airlifted from Cordelia's neighborhood.

"It's a lot nicer than I expected," Benji said.

"See?" Cordelia said. "I told you it wouldn't be so bad."

"We haven't gone inside any of the houses yet."

They entered the main office. Everything had been artfully arranged like a showroom in a furniture store. A diffuser sent plumes of lavender-scented mist into the air. On the wall above a stone fireplace, the words *Shady Rest* were pieced together from stained strips of wood.

A young woman wearing a business suit looked up from a tablet as they entered.

"Welcome, friends!" she exclaimed, enthusiastically shaking their hands. "My name is Trisha Williams, but you can call me Trish. Everyone does!" She took a moment to point to each of them. "And you are Cordelia, Benji, and Agnes. Correct? Ms. Knox is so excited to give you the full Shady Rest experience today. Follow me, please. Isn't this weather invigorating? There's nothing better than a winter morning to get the heart pumping. . . ."

Trish, who seemed to view silence as some sort of enemy that needed to be vanquished at every step, led them deeper into the house. Several rooms had been designated as offices. Through the glass doors, Cordelia saw employees going about their business: a few talking on a phone or working at a computer, one adding *24 Spruce Mill Lane* to a list of addresses on a dry-erase board. In one room, a man with a concerned look on his face nodded in understanding while a well-dressed couple took turns talking. As Cordelia turned the corner, she saw the man reach for a tissue and hand it across his desk.

"Here we are," Trish said, opening a pair of double doors. "Ms. Knox will be with you in just a moment. There are chocolate-chip muffins and water on the table."

They entered a meeting room with a lot of plaques and framed newspaper articles on the walls. The headlines were all riffs on a common theme: LELAND KNOX GIVES SOMEONE A BUNCH OF MONEY. The causes varied greatly—a school in a Bolivian village, a soup kitchen in Detroit, a local bookstore on the verge of bankruptcy—but the photo ops were always the same: a man with a bow tie and front-page smile posing with a grateful beneficiary.

"That's my grandfather," said Laurel, entering the room and catching them looking at the articles. "Leland Knox. He was a great man. Made his fortune early and spent the rest of his life giving it away. You name the charity, and I promise they have a check with his name on it. He died last summer."

"I'm sorry," Cordelia said.

Laurel gave a tiny shrug. "He left the world a better place, which was all he ever wanted. Shady Rest was his brainchild, and I hope to continue his legacy. Sit, sit. We have a lot to talk about."

Cordelia took a seat. Laurel gave her a giddy smile, as though she had been waiting for this moment her entire life. She was wearing a scoop-necked black top, designer jeans, and a gold ankh. Her knee-high boots looked fresh from the box. It was a cool outfit, and Laurel looked good in it. Cordelia could imagine wearing something like it when she was older.

When everyone had settled in, Laurel tapped her watch and a screen lowered itself from the ceiling.

"I have a video to show you. We made it for clients who come to us for help but have trouble grasping what we do here. It might be a good place to start."

The lights dimmed.

Jaunty piano music started to play, and an animated haunted house with dark windows and tall gables appeared on the screen. A bolt of lightning struck the weather vane on the roof, and the walls suddenly turned transparent, revealing a cute ghost with big eyes and a friendly smile.

"Aww," said Cordelia.

"Our business has several steps," Laurel said. "The first is identifying 'at risk' spirits. In other words, ghosts whose haunts are in danger of being destroyed."

The music grew more ominous as a crane wielding a wrecking ball with demonic eyes pulled to the curb. Inside the house, the cute ghost cowered with fear, peeking through a window as the giant ball swung back and forth, warming up for the destruction to come. Right before it struck, however, a white van with *SHADY REST* emblazoned on the side screeched to a halt, blocking its path. The doors of the van flew open, and from it emerged a large man carrying a duffel bag, and a pretty, auburn-haired woman. (Cordelia glanced at Laurel, who gave an embarrassed shrug.) The pair ran into the house, which returned to its original, nontransparent mode. A few moments passed, during which the crane driver impatiently puffed on a cigar, and then the windows of the house exploded with indigo light. The heroes of Shady Rest exited the front door. In the woman's arms was the cute ghost, cuddled up in a tube like a baby.

As the van pulled away, the wrecking ball knocked the haunted house to smithereens.

"Once we've determined a haunting is legitimate," Laurel said, "we capture the ghost, just like you saw me and Kyle do in Gideon's Ark. The spirit is then placed into a storage facility while we rebuild the ghost's house from scratch right here in the village." This played out on the screen, as workers wearing *SHADY REST* T-shirts built an identical house in a matter of seconds. "If at all possible, we prefer using the original blueprints. We had issues early on when we tried to modernize the plans. For reasons we don't fully understand, the architecture of these houses seems tied to their . . . hauntability."

Cordelia thought Laurel would be very interested in archimancy. But that could wait for now. Today was about getting answers, not giving them.

"What happens after the ghosts move into their new homes?" Cordelia asked.

"They stay there. Forever. We've rescued forty-three ghosts so far. And built forty-three haunted houses to match."

"Can we see the ghosts?" Cordelia asked.

Laurel grinned. "That's why you're here."

The Tour

They drove through the village. Each house was vastly different from the one next to it, creating some unlikely neighbors: a log cabin and an ultra-modern glass house, a lavish mansion and a one-room cottage. Only their front yards were identical, a landscape of neatly trimmed lawns devoid of bushes or flowers. There were no cars in the driveways, no toys in the backyard.

No sign of life at all.

They parked in front of a squat brick house. As they walked up the front path, Cordelia was surprised to hear a dozen different voices talking at once, as though there were a party going on inside the house.

"I thought ghosts couldn't talk," Agnes whispered to Cordelia.

"We're not in Shadow School anymore. Maybe things are different here."

As soon as they entered the house, however, Cordelia saw that the voices were not ghostly in origin. On almost every wall, loud videos were playing on flat screens like the one Laurel had used to subdue Seamus Gideon. These weren't movies or TV shows, but a catalog of personal memories captured by phone: vacations, school concerts, cats, dogs, various people blowing out various candles. In the one nearest Cordelia, a baby giggled while an unseen playmate clapped her hands and made silly sounds offscreen.

"I didn't want our ghosts to feel lonely," Laurel said. "So in each house, we've patched into the social-media feeds of all the people they left behind. This way they can see what everyone is up to and still feel like they're part of the world. We call them 'life windows.'"

Benji made an exploding noise and threw his hands out from his head: *Mind blown.* "So they binge-watch their friends and family all day long? It's like Netflix for ghosts."

Cordelia asked, "Doesn't it make them sad, seeing

all the fun that everyone else is having without them?"

Laurel regarded Cordelia with a thoughtful expression. "The first thing you think about is the ghosts' feelings. My grandfather would have loved you. How's this? I'll introduce you to Dr. Gill. You can tell me yourself if she's happy or not."

They walked through the house, the floor squeaking at the unanticipated weight of corporeal visitors. Benji shivered beneath his hoodie. "Sorry it's so cold in here," Laurel said, blowing into her hands. "No use wasting money on heat when there's no one here to appreciate it." This wasn't the only place where corners had been cut. The walls had been primed but not painted. There was barely any furniture. The appliances were cardboard models. Overall, it felt more like the set of a play than an actual home.

And everywhere—*everywhere*—were the life windows. Cordelia felt like she was in an appliance store shopping for a new TV.

She feigned interest in some kid's high school graduation speech until Laurel entered the next room, then Cordelia reached into her pocket and slipped the spectercles over her head. The dizziness wasn't as bad as it had been in the ark. Hopefully this meant her eyes were adjusting.

"That's a good look for you," Benji whispered with a

barely suppressed grin. Cordelia stuck out her tongue. As if needing the spectercles in the first place wasn't humiliating enough, they made her look like she had giant bug eyes.

She followed the rest of the group into the master bedroom. A hazy pink shape was sitting on the edge of the bed. Cordelia blinked a few times until the image settled into that of an older woman wearing a fuzzy robe. Her feet were bare, and there was a white towel wound around her head. All her attention was riveted on the life window across from her. This footage was grainier than the other samples Cordelia had seen around the house—taken from a time when people had used actual video cameras and not their phones. In it, a wedding couple was dancing, the bride's head nestled against the groom's shoulder.

"Judging from the looks on your faces, I'm guessing Dr. Gill is sitting right there," Laurel said, pointing to the bed. "I'm not surprised. This is her favorite spot. She also likes to watch the toothpaste commercials downstairs." The kids looked at her in bewilderment, and Laurel added, "Dr. Gill was a dentist for forty years."

Benji knelt down and assessed the ghost. "She looks happy enough."

Cordelia would have said "mesmerized," but there was no denying the faint smile on the ghost's lips.

"That's Dr. Gill in the video, isn't it?"

Laurel nodded. "Her husband posted it on the anniversary of her death. He's a dentist as well—still practicing, believe it or not." On the video, the couple was feeding each other from a cake shaped like a giant molar. "Dr. Gill was haunting the old office they used to share, which was due to be demolished. We rescued her just in time."

Cordelia loved that word: *rescued*. Sure, there weren't any Brightkeys involved, but if Laurel hadn't intervened, Dr. Gill's spirit would have been lost forever. *And Laurel can't even see them*, Cordelia thought. *Imagine how many ghosts we could rescue together!*

Maybe Shadow School didn't need her anymore, but Shady Rest did.

"Show us more," Cordelia said.

Over the next hour, they traversed the empty streets of the village and visited four different houses. Each was haunted by a single ghost. Three of the spirits were older and seemed at peace, having enjoyed their full allotment of years on Earth. The fourth resident was a young man who would never graduate from the college he had been attending at the time of his death. If he felt cheated by his untimely demise, however, he didn't show it. Like his older brethren, he seemed content to roam the halls of his manufactured haunt, staring at the recorded memories of his life (including many video-game streams) and watching the lives of his loved ones continue without him.

Around noon, they returned to the conference room, where an elaborate lunch had been set out on the table: several sandwich choices cut into neat triangles, a variety of salads, and freshly baked chocolate-chip cookies. The moment the kids sat down, Trish ran into the room with mugs of hot cocoa topped with whipped cream and cinnamon.

"So, what do you think?" Laurel asked as everyone started to eat.

"This is the most amazing place I've ever seen in my life," Cordelia said. "You're like a ghost conservationist!"

Laurel looked pleased. "That's exactly how Grandpa used to describe it. 'Some people save pandas. We save ghosts!'"

"You should put that on a T-shirt," Benji said.

"I'd love to, but it's crucial that Shady Rest remain under the radar. I trust the three of you can keep everything you've seen today to yourself? You can't even tell your parents."

The kids nodded. They were used to keeping secrets.

"Are you afraid people won't believe you?" Cordelia asked.

"That's part of it. I can't say I even blame them. It's hard to believe what you can't see with your own eyes. But Grandpa was also afraid of other companies stealing our system in order to turn a profit."

"How?" Benji asked. "Ghosts don't have money."

"But their relatives do. Imagine knowing the spirit of your beloved grandmother was about to blink out forever because her house was due to be demolished. How much would you pay to move her somewhere safe? That's just one example. There are a lot of ways for other people to monetize what we do here. I don't want that to happen."

"But you must make money somehow," Agnes said, perhaps remembering Mr. Shadow's comments earlier that week. "Otherwise how are you able to build new houses? Or pay the people who work here?"

"Her gramps probably left her a boatload of cash," Benji said.

"Benji!" Cordelia exclaimed.

"What?"

"It's okay," Laurel said, though the smile had faded from her lips. It was clear she had been close to her grandfather, and his death probably still weighed heavily on her mind. "Believe it or not, Grandpa died a penniless man. I inherited Shady Rest, but that's it. We do have some income flow, though. Occasionally homeowners ask us to remove a troublesome spirit, and we take a minimal fee. No more than we need, of course."

A sudden thought struck Cordelia. "You're not going to rebuild Gideon's entire ark, are you?"

Laurel laughed. "There's no need. Any 'hauntable' house will work—it's not specific to the ghost. Grandpa insisted on rebuilding each spirit's personal haunt, but I don't see the purpose when we know of several simple house plans that will work for any ghost. We'll use one of those for Gideon." Laurel took a nibble of her sandwich. "It was such a stroke of luck you were at the ark that day. We wouldn't have been able to catch Gideon otherwise. We make a good team."

"It wasn't luck," Cordelia said. "It was fate."

Laurel raised her mug. "Even better."

"Wait a sec," Agnes said. "If you need someone with the Sight, then how did you catch all the ghosts that are already here?"

Laurel nodded, as though this was something she had meant to mention but overlooked. "We did employ a young man named Victor who could see the ghosts, just like you two. He helped Grandpa for years. It's because of him that we were able to save the ones we did. But he's been gone for nearly six months now, and I'm afraid our entire endeavor has ground to a halt without him."

The color drained from Benji's face. "He died?"

Laurel nearly spit out her cocoa. "No! Of course not! He just quit. Not everyone is cut out for this. Victor was tired of seeing ghosts every day. He wanted a normal life."

Benji said, "I can understand that."

"So what do you think?" Laurel asked. "Would you three like to join the staff of Shady Rest? We could really use your help. Benji and Cordelia, for your amazing talent, and Agnes—I was thinking I could teach you how to work the equipment."

"I'm totally and completely in," said Cordelia.

"I'm game too," said Agnes.

The girls turned to Benji.

"Sorry," he said. "It's cool what you've done here. And I won't tell anybody what I've seen today. But I don't want any part of this."

"Because it's dangerous?" Laurel asked. "Don't go by what happened at the ark. I would never allow you anywhere near a phantom. Besides, Kyle and I will be doing the actual capturing. You just need to point us in the right direction."

"My answer's still no," Benji said.

"Don't you want to think about it first?" Cordelia asked.

"No need. I really hope you and Agnes like it here. But I've made my decision, and there's nothing you can do to change my mind."

"I understand," Laurel said. She broke off a piece of a chocolate-chip cookie. "One last thing, though. I would, of course, be paying you for your service—something commensurate with your unique abilities. If that kind of thing matters to you."

Benji ran a hand through his hair, no doubt thinking about how badly his family could use the money. Finally, he smiled.

"How much?" he asked.

9

Learning the Ropes

They returned to Shady Rest the following Saturday for more "volunteering." Since this was going to be a weekly routine, their parents decided to divvy up the driving tasks. This week, it was Mrs. Núñez's turn. Benji's mom usually loved to chat with the girls, but today she barely said a word. It was like some vital light inside her had been extinguished. Cordelia wished there was something she could do to help, but the concerns that haunted her distant gaze were real, grown-up problems. There was no Brightkey to fix them.

Trish was talking on the phone when they entered the main office. Now that the kids were officially employed by Shady Rest, she greeted them with complete indifference, as though her initial friendliness had been a show for their benefit. When the kids continued to stand there, waiting for directions, she gave them an annoyed look and turned away. Her phone conversation definitely wasn't work related, unless work involved a "hottie" named Josh who had just moved into Trish's apartment building. Cordelia caught a glimpse of Laurel as she entered one of the interior offices and decided it would be easier to approach her directly instead of waiting for Trish. She crossed the lobby and peeked her head through the open door. A younger guy with a goatee and slicked-back hair was showing Laurel something on an iPad. Cordelia could smell his cologne from where she was standing.

". . . at the size of this place," he said. "It looks like a castle! This is a prime choice, Ms. Knox. A prime choice."

"Has Kenny run background yet?"

"Yup. A maid died on the premises back in 1972."

"That sounds promising. But only if–"

"Dozens of sightings throughout the years. That's more than enough to establish . . ."

The man noticed Cordelia standing at the door.

"Hey!" he barked. "Get out of here, kid!"

"Carl," Laurel said with a warning tone in her voice.

"This is Cordelia Liu. She's one of the new Victors."

Carl looked immediately repentant.

"Sorry," he said. "I didn't know. Welcome to Shady Rest."

"Thanks," Cordelia said. "I couldn't help but overhear. Are we going to help the ghost of that maid?"

"Not today," Laurel said. "Come on. We've got a long drive in front of us."

They headed back into the lobby. On the way out the front door, Laurel gave Trish a withering look. Cordelia suspected the receptionist's cell-phone usage during work hours would be addressed sometime soon.

"Every Saturday, you'll be doing one of two things," Laurel said, wrapping a beautiful cashmere scarf around her neck. "The first is going from house to house and checking on the ghosts. Victor called it 'visiting hours.'"

"Why would we need to check on them?" Benji asked.

"We'll get to that next week," Laurel said. "Today we're going out into the field—which is your second responsibility. We have a long backlog of ghosts we need to capture. A lot of their haunts are due to be demolished in the next few weeks, so these are literal rescue missions."

"Sounds like fun!" Cordelia said.

They followed Laurel along a narrow driveway that

ran behind the main office. Kyle was loading equipment from a large shed into a white van with *PDO Contractors* emblazoned on the side. The van was already running, chugging gray puffs of smoke into the air.

Kyle opened the side door. "In you go," he said, gesturing for the children to enter. "Don't get me killed, and we should all get along fine."

The kids slid into the back seat while Kyle and Laurel got in front. Cordelia took a peek at the cargo bay, where all sorts of equipment were secured with thick rope: the long duffel bag from the ark, a cooler, several toolboxes, a canister that looked like something a scuba diver might wear, and a rather large—and hence somewhat ominous—first-aid kit. The majority of the space, however, was taken up by a stainless-steel machine that had been bolted to the floor. It hummed like a refrigerator.

Kyle drove them past the guardhouse and onto the main road.

"Why does the van say 'PDO Contractors'?" Agnes asked.

"My old business," Kyle said with a nostalgic look in his eyes. "We were making a pretty good run of it until my partner starting stealing stuff from the houses we were supposed to be fixing." Kyle kept one hand on the steering wheel and used the other to turn the knob of the radio, navigating an ocean of white noise. "After he got arrested, I tried to run things by myself for a while, but it didn't work out. Lost everything except the van."

"What's the 'PDO' stand for?" Cordelia asked.

Kyle hesitated. "Something stupid. I don't even remember."

This brief exchange included more words, in total, than Kyle had spoken since they'd met. Perhaps thinking that this constituted some sort of breakthrough in their relationship, Benji leaned forward and offered Kyle his phone. "Come on, dude. No one uses the radio anymore. You can play anything you want through this."

Kyle gave the phone a look of disgust and continued to fiddle with the tuning knob.

"Static's cool too," Benji said.

"This first job's a layup," said Laurel. "Ancient farmhouse out by Pawtuckaway Lake. The current owner is a developer who wants to knock the entire thing to the ground and use the land to build something he can turn a profit on. He wasn't going to let us come at first—why should he care if the house is haunted when he's going to demolish it anyway? But then we warned him that if we didn't capture the ghost, it was going to stick around and haunt the new house he built—which would definitely hurt his chances of selling it."

"But that's not true," Agnes said.

"I think it's okay to bend the truth if it's for a good cause."

"Me too," said Cordelia. She had often used the same logic to justify lying to her parents, so it was gratifying to hear an actual grown-up voice her agreement.

Agnes asked, "How did the owner know the house was haunted to begin with?"

"The usual clues," Laurel said. "Lights flashing, doors slamming. A sudden, inexplicable drop in temperature. A ghost can definitely make its presence felt, even to those without the Sight. Kyle and I have experienced things that would make your spine twist into a knot. In some ways, it's probably even scarier because we can't see them." Her gaze passed between Cordelia and Benji. "Though that must be hard for you two to imagine."

Cordelia remembered those early moments in the ark before she put on the spectercles. "Not so hard," she said.

After a long stretch of empty country roads, they pulled up to a farmhouse set against the withered stalks of an abandoned cornfield. The house was a faded shade of red with a decapitated chimney and stone-shattered windows. Black liquid dripped from the gutters and collected in a dank stream that ran across the front yard like a polluted moat.

The three kids piled out of the van.

"Sweet pad," Benji said.

"You two head inside and do reconnaissance," Laurel said, opening the back doors of the van so they could unload the equipment. "We'll be right behind you."

"What do we do if we find the ghost?" Benji asked.

"Nothing. Just wait until we get there."

The inside of the house wasn't any nicer than the outside. Most of the furniture had been left to rot like organs inside a decomposing corpse. A potted fern had gone feral, stretching its leafy arms across half the living room.

Cordelia put the spectercles on and the room instantly began to spin. She leaned against the wall, closing her eyes until it passed.

"What's the name of that ride?" Cordelia asked. "Where you stick to the walls because it's spinning so fast?"

"The Gravitron! I love that one!"

"I used to."

The farmhouse wasn't large, and after a quick search of the first floor, they went up a set of rickety stairs. A dark hallway offered them three options. Cordelia started to open the closest door when she was struck by a wave of dizziness, as though she had just been spinning around in circles and was now trying to walk straight. A flat surface was approaching fast—either the floor or a wall; it was impossible to tell—and Cordelia would have struck it hard were it not for Benji's amazing reflexes. She felt his arms around her shoulders, holding her still.

"Whoa!" he said. "You okay?"

Cordelia nodded. The dizziness had passed, at least for now, leaving her free to realize how close Benji was standing. She could feel his warm breath against her cheek.

"Thanks," she said, stepping away. "I guess my eyes needed a little more time to adjust to the spectercles."

"Has something like that happened before?"

It hadn't. After the initial period of adjustment, the spectercles had always worked fine. This random bout of dizziness was a new twist, and Cordelia didn't like it. She wasn't about to let Benji know that, however. Benji with his stupid, flawless Sight.

"It's nothing to worry about," she said.

Cordelia tried opening the door again, this time without any ill effects, and entered a small office. There was a metal desk with an old, boxy computer on it, a bookcase packed with paperback westerns, and a scarecrow holding a Kramer Farm's World-Famous Corn Maze sign. Behind the scarecrow, an array of hand-drawn maps had been displayed to commemorate twenty-five years of mazes. Each design was a unique work of art, a testament to its creator's passion and care.

The ghost was on the couch. He was a man in his sixties wearing a flannel shirt, his chin perched on folded hands as he regarded a set of toothpicks that had been arranged like a maze in front of him. There was an intense look of concentration on his face, like a chess player planning his next move.

"Guess this must be Mr. Kramer," Benji said. "Still thinking about his mazes. That's dedication." The ghost tilted his head, as though hearing an interesting sound in the distance, and the smile vanished from Benji's face. "Let's keep our distance. After what happened in the ark–"

Cordelia took a seat on the couch.

"Or you could just . . . sit next to him," Benji said. "He looks sad."

"He's dead. That's got to affect your mood some. Come on, Cord–let's go downstairs."

"In a minute. I want to explain what's going on so he doesn't get scared." Cordelia folded her legs beneath her and turned to face the ghost. "Sorry to intrude, Mr. Kramer, but this place isn't safe for you anymore. We're going to use a special machine to take you somewhere new. It won't hurt"–Cordelia hoped that was true–"and when you wake up you'll be in a brand-new house where you'll get to see your loved ones again. Sort of."

Cordelia searched Mr. Kramer's face for any reaction. His unblinking gaze didn't move from the toothpicks, but she thought his features had softened a bit, as though he were more at peace than before. That was probably just wishful thinking on her part, however. More than likely, the ghost hadn't registered a single thing she said.

Laurel and Agnes entered the room. Kyle dropped the duffel bag to the floor, shattering the calm with a rude clang.

"You find the ghost yet?" Laurel asked.

"I'm sitting next to him."

Laurel gave Cordelia a curious look. "You're really not scared of them at all, are you?"

Benji said, "Yet put a centipede next to her and she screams her head off."

"Nothing should have that many legs," Cordelia muttered.

"What's it doing?" Kyle asked, looking in the ghost's general vicinity.

"Nothing," Cordelia said. "Just staring at the table, like he's in a daze."

Laurel and Kyle exchanged a smile.

"Our favorite type of ghost," Laurel explained.

"Some of them never stop moving. That's why we have to use the video screens to mesmerize them. But others just sit there like they're in a coma or something. Makes catching them a breeze. Victor used to call them 'roses.'"

Kyle chuckled and added, "'A beautiful flower that we can replant somewhere new, where it can grow safe and strong again.'" It was a higher-pitched voice than his own, no doubt an imitation of Victor's, with an edge of mockery that made both Laurel and Kyle burst into laughter.

"Sounds like Victor really liked the ghosts," Agnes said.

"Oh, he *loved* them," said Kyle, still chuckling. "He could go on and on for—"

"But you said he quit because he was tired of them," Agnes said.

The laughter stopped. Laurel gave Agnes an annoyed look, like a teacher corrected by a student.

"Well . . . he did love the ghosts at first," Laurel said. "Then he changed his mind."

"Did something happen?" Cordelia asked.

"Nothing in particular. Guess he'd just had enough."

Kyle started to add something, but Cordelia saw Laurel shoot him a quick warning glance: *Don't open your mouth.* He knelt down and unzipped the duffel bag instead. Laurel was clearly afraid that Kyle might reveal some secret she wanted to keep from the children. Cordelia's paranoia kicked into full gear for a moment—*What are they hiding about Victor? We have to find out!*—before she reminded herself that grown-ups kept perfectly innocuous secrets from children all the time, usually "for their own good." If Laurel didn't want to tell them something, she probably had a good reason. She had saved them from a phantom. She ran a whole business dedicated to helping ghosts.

Cordelia could trust her.

While Agnes helped set up the equipment, Cordelia and Benji waited in the living room. Without a task to distract them, they found themselves awkward in each other's company, their conversation stuttering and stalling like an old engine in need of repair. Those moments in the ark where he had, more or less, confessed his feelings, and she had, more or less, blown him off, colored every look between them. Part of her wished it had never happened. Part of her wanted him to ask her out again.

"I know you don't want to be here," Cordelia finally said. "But I think it's really sweet that you're doing this for your family."

"Yeah, thanks. This pays a lot more than bagging

groceries." Benji gave her a shy smile. "And I guess spending every Saturday with you isn't totally awful. Even if you do kind of look like a praying mantis."

"What?" Cordelia asked, then realized that she was still wearing the spectercles. She yanked them off, cheeks flushed with embarrassment, just as Laurel came downstairs holding a brass tube identical to the one she had used in the ark. The only difference was the mist swirling within it. Mr. Kramer's essence was not ocean blue, as Gideon's had been, but the rich brown of freshly tilled soil.

They returned to the van. Laurel opened the back doors and pressed a button on the stainless-steel machine bolted to the floor. The front of it slid open like something out of a sci-fi movie. Plumes of thick mist rose from the interior.

"Is that a liquid-nitrogen freezer?" Agnes asked, with the same tone of delighted disbelief another girl might have used upon spotting her celebrity crush walking down the street.

Laurel nodded. "Have you ever seen one up close before?"

"Only in my dreams."

"This one's just a baby. I'll have to show you our main unit back at the village. That one will knock your socks off."

"Better not," Benji said. "Agnes might pass out from excitement."

"What do you use it for?" Cordelia asked.

"Hold this," Laurel said, handing her the tube. Cordelia gasped in surprise. Even through her thick gloves, she could feel its heat.

"It's warm," Cordelia said, handing it to Agnes.

"For now," replied Laurel. She removed a pair of elbow-length rubber gloves from a side compartment and started to pull them on. "In ten minutes, the boo-tube will be too scalding to hold. In thirty minutes, it'll burn the flesh from your fingers. In an hour, the glass window will shatter, and the ghost will be free again."

For a moment, the kids stared at Laurel in disbelief. Then Benji burst into laughter.

"Boo-tube?" he asked.

"Its technical name is long and difficult to pronounce."

"So you went with *boo-tube* instead?"

"You're missing the point! After we capture the ghosts, they start heating up. If we don't reduce their temperature, the entire tube will start melting in about an hour. And then they're back out in the world again."

"Makes sense," Agnes said. "Ghosts are pure energy, right? How else would they be able to do things like make lights flicker and slam doors? That isn't a problem in a house, where those excited molecules have plenty of room to spread out. But compressing all that energy into an area of, what"—Agnes took stock of the boo-tube—"fifteen hundred cubic centimeters? That's like trying to stuff a bonfire into a fireplace."

Laurel looked impressed. "You're pretty smart for a kid."

"I can bake too."

After Laurel had finished securing the boo-tube inside the freezer, they all climbed into the van.

"That didn't take as long as I thought it would," Benji said. "We'll be back home by lunch!"

Laurel turned in her seat and gave him a smile. "You didn't think we were done, did you?"

10

Visiting Hours

They captured two more ghosts after leaving Mr. Kramer's house. The first was a salesman type wearing a canary-yellow sports jacket, who kept mouthing words into an invisible phone while pacing the floor. The second ghost was a "rose" making knitting motions with her hands. The boo-mists of the two ghosts were as different as could be. The man's mist polluted the tube, like exhaust fumes from an old car, while the woman's resembled the steam from a teakettle.

"I wish I could see the mists for myself," Agnes said that Monday as they ate lunch. "But from what you've told me, I think the color reveals the essence of each person. Gideon's was blue because he dreamed of sailing the ocean in his ark, and Mr. Kramer's was brown because he was a farmer."

Benji said, "It's different for each ghost. Like the Brights."

Cordelia nodded. She was quieter than usual, content to listen. *This is the way it's supposed to be,* she thought, unable to keep the grin off her face. *The three of us, helping the ghosts. Together.*

There had clearly been something bothering Agnes all day, however, and as they gathered their things to go to fifth period, she finally aired it. "Saturday was fun, but I'm still a little iffy about this whole deal. I think they're hiding something from us."

Benji scoffed. "*Hiding* something? They literally gave us a tour, Ag! We know what they're doing, who's doing it, why they're doing it, and how they're doing it!"

Cordelia agreed with Benji, though she was surprised to hear him come to the defense of Shady Rest so quickly.

"Listen, I'm not saying they're evil or anything," Agnes said. "I researched Mr. Knox, and there's no denying that he's done a lot of good in the world."

"See?" Benji said.

"But Mr. Knox isn't running Shady Rest anymore. I'm not as sold on his granddaughter. I couldn't find anything about her online, outside of some old articles about her high school track team. Apparently she was an amazing long-distance runner. After that, she drops off the map completely."

"Maybe she's just private," Cordelia suggested.

"Maybe. And it does seem like they're helping the ghosts, so that's good. But you have to admit it's a pretty weird coincidence that they were at the ark that day. Two ghost catchers *happen* to be at a place a phantom *happens* to appear, when two kids with the Sight *happen* to be there too? Oh—and the ghost catchers *happen* to be desperately searching for someone with the Sight in order to run their business?"

Cordelia gave a begrudging nod. "That's a lot of 'happens.'" Maybe Agnes was right, and she was willing to overlook all these red flags because she wanted everything to work out with Shady Rest. The mere thought of quitting tied her stomach in knots. After being teased with a chance to help the ghosts in this new and exciting way, Cordelia couldn't go back to feeling useless again. She just couldn't.

"Okay," Benji said. "Let's say it wasn't a coincidence. What was it?"

Agnes twisted her braid. "I'm not sure exactly. All I know is Laurel lost the only employee she had who could see the ghosts. She can't run her business without one. And the way events worked out, she got not one, but two replacements. That just seems . . . oddly seren-dipitous."

"Seren-what?" Benji asked.

"Fortunate. Sorry—my mom got me SAT flash cards for Christmas again."

"It just doesn't make any sense, Agnes," Cordelia said, working it through. "Even if what happened at Shady Rest was some kind of setup—which is impossible, by the way, unless Laurel can magically control phantoms—why bother going through all that trouble? If Laurel knew that me and Benji had the Sight, and wanted us to work for her, all she had to do was ask. Easy."

"You're right," Agnes said. "I don't have an expla-nation that makes sense. I'm just saying it's a big coincidence."

Cordelia and Benji guided Agnes around a ghost with loose jeans hanging low on his hips and unlaced sneakers. He gave them a nod as the dehaunter pulled him through the ceiling.

"Coincidences happen, Ag," Benji said. "And maybe it's fate, like Cordelia said. The money I'm making at Shady Rest is really going to help my family. I told my parents yesterday that I'd been bagging groceries and shoveling driveways all over town, and I wanted to chip in until things get better. They didn't want to take my money at first, but I talked them into it. It's not enough to fix everything, but it's something. My mom sang while she was cooking dinner. Do you know how long it's been since she did that?"

"I'm glad things are better," Cordelia said.

"It's not just the ark," Agnes said. "I feel like they get a little weird whenever Victor's name comes up. Like maybe he quit because something bad happened, and they don't want to tell us because it might scare us away."

"So they're not telling us everything," Benji said. "Who cares? Let's focus on what we know. The guy who created Shady Rest was a saint, his granddaughter literally rescued us from a phantom, and we've seen firsthand evidence that their company is helping ghosts. Any way you look at it, we're on the same side. And it's not like we haven't been keeping secrets of our own." Benji waved his arms, encompassing the entirety of Shadow School. "Haunted school . . . Brightkeys . . . dehaunter. Just because they're hiding a few things doesn't make them bad. It just means they're cautious, like us."

"You're probably right," Agnes said. "But we should keep our guards up, just in case."

"Don't we always?" asked Cordelia.

◆ ◆ ◆

That Saturday it was Ms. Matheson's turn to drive. Cordelia wasn't crazy about Agnes's mother, a professor at an online university who often railed against "children today" not taking the issues of the world seriously enough. It was an awkward ride. Instead of music, Ms. Matheson blasted some sort of boring talk show on NPR and glared at the kids whenever they started a conversation, as though they were hitchhikers who should have been more grateful for the ride.

At least she drove fast. They arrived at Shady Rest in record time, and Trish, whose cell phone was noticeably absent, directed them to the equipment shed. They saw Laurel in the back and walked past shelves filled with empty boo-tubes and electronic gizmos. Agnes paused to fiddle with the switches of a long black machine.

"What's this do?" she asked.

"Nothing," Laurel said. "It's a failed prototype of the ghost catcher we currently use."

"How about this one?" Agnes asked, poking the machine next to it.

"I promise I'll give you a complete tour at some point. But right now I need to explain what you're doing today."

Agnes reluctantly left the machines behind and joined the rest of the group at the back of the shed. Her eyes kept straying to the shelves behind them, though. Cordelia bit back a smile.

"Your job is to visit as many houses as possible today and check in on the residents," Laurel said, tossing Cordelia a set of keys. "Each one of these is labeled with a street name. All the houses on that street share the same key. Just makes it easier."

"Why lock them at all?" Benji asked. "It's not like the ghosts can escape."

"A simple precaution against thieves and vandals, just in case anyone sneaks past the guardhouse. Those life windows are expensive." She handed Agnes an iPad. "You're in charge of this. There's an app with a map of the village. Each individual house is represented by a tiny icon. As you make visual confirmation of each ghost, just tap on the house. It saves automatically." She indicated a long bike rack to her left. "Take any one you like. I'd drive you myself, but I have an important meeting this morning about potential sites."

"Sounds easy enough," Benji said, eagerly eyeing the bikes.

"I don't get it," Agnes said. "The ghosts literally can't leave. What's the point of checking on them?"

Laurel's smile seemed a little forced. "Wow, Agnes. You're always thinking, aren't you? I was just about to get to that. If you tap on the house twice, it'll bring you to a menu where you can let maintenance know about any issues. If you see any structural damage, for example, or maybe one of the life windows is malfunctioning. This way my people know to fix it."

"Can't your staff search for problems like that?" Agnes asked.

"Going inside the houses makes them a little uneasy. I try to limit it as much as possible."

"That makes sense," Cordelia said.

"Let me show you something else," Laurel said. She took the iPad out of Agnes's hands and brought up the map. "See this red circle up here? That's what you tap if you see any of the ghosts glowing. Victor said blue was the most common color, but he also saw gold and silver and even pink once. The color doesn't matter. It's the glowing we care about. Let us know right away and wait for Kyle and me to get there."

Benji looked up from adjusting the seat of a nifty-looking ten-speed. "We have glowing ghosts now? What's that all about?"

"It's perfectly natural," Laurel said. "Ghosts have a kind of . . . life cycle, I guess you'd call it. Or death cycle. Normal ghosts like Dr. Gill will eventually change to bad, more powerful ones like Gideon."

"You called that kind . . . phantoms, right?" Cordelia

asked, trying to give the impression that this was all new to her.

"That's right. There's nothing we can do to stop a ghost's inevitable transformation. You might as well ask a butterfly to stay in its cocoon. But when a ghost starts to glow, it's like a warning signal that it's on the verge of turning. If you tell us, we can freeze the spirit in a boo-tube before it gets dangerous."

"What happens if we go into a house and a ghost has already turned into a phantom?" Benji asked.

"Leave," Laurel said. "That reminds me—there's actually one house where that happened. A ghost turned into a particularly nasty phantom, and we decided it was just easier to lock the door and leave it be." She turned the tablet toward them and zoomed in on 14 Willow Drive. "There it is. The very first house Grandpa ever built—purple, believe it or not. Gorgeous place. That phantom, though . . ." Her face drained of color. "There are some ghosts that are beyond our help. Whatever you do, don't go in there. You'll never come out again."

"Good to know," Cordelia said.

They started with the three houses down the road from the main office. The ranch. The log cabin. The split-level. Inside, they were all the same. The air was cold and stale, like a vacation home left unoccupied for months.

On almost every wall hung a life window, blasting memories at high volume.

According to Laurel, there was a special team that curated videos to meet the specific needs of each inhabitant. These included everything from social-media feeds and home videos to TV shows and sporting events. Sometimes information about a ghost was scarce, or the spirit had died a long time ago. In that case, more generic videos were used, as Laurel had done with Gideon: nature scenes, cooking videos, cats. Anything, Cordelia supposed, to make the ghosts feel more alive.

The life windows certainly made finding the ghosts easier: They were always standing in front of one screen or another, watching the images with a slack-jawed expression. Once Cordelia or Benji spotted a ghost, Agnes tapped the appropriate icon on the tablet, the app rewarded them with an encouraging *ding*, and they continued to their next destination.

The first few houses were fun. After that, it started to feel like work. The low point was when Cordelia suffered another attack of dizziness, though luckily she was able to hide it from her friends by falling onto a convenient couch until it passed.

By noon, the novelty of the job had worn off completely. They were getting bored.

"It's like playing hide-and-seek with someone who doesn't understand the rules," Benji said. "Why don't we take a break and ride to the edge of the property? We can work our way back from there."

It was relatively warm for early February, and the fresh air felt invigorating. Cordelia's bike was brand-new and fancier than the one she had at home, with lots of knobs that she was afraid to touch. It worked great, though. She pumped the pedals and darted down the street. There was no need to worry about traffic. There were no cars.

"This place gives me the creeps," Agnes said. "It's so quiet."

"Yeah," said Benji. "It's a real ghost town."

The two girls rolled their eyes.

"What? Someone had to say it!"

They entered a new section of the village that Laurel hadn't shown them on their tour. There was no architectural variety here. Each house was exactly the same: a tiny white ranch with black shutters. The only way to tell them apart was the number spray-painted on each door.

"Is this where the poor ghosts live?" Benji asked.

"Laurel said they needed a haunt, not necessarily

105

their haunt," Agnes said as they cycled past a long row of the identical houses. There was barely any space between them. "I'm sure the archimancy works fine, even if it's not much to look at."

"Makes sense to me," Benji said. "Why spend all that money on a big fancy house? It's not like the ghosts know the difference. They have to cut corners somewhere if they want to keep doing this."

"I still like the other section better," Cordelia said.

They parked their bikes and got to work. Searching the smaller houses was a breeze, and the kids were able to blow through an entire block in less than an hour. To break the monotony, they started making predictions before they opened each door: Would the ghost be male or female? Young or old? Found on the first or second floor? Agnes guessed correctly far more often than the others, making Cordelia think that what she lacked in Sight, she made up for in psychic ability.

There was one house, however, where all their guesses were wrong, because there was no ghost inside it—or even life windows, for that matter. Instead, a dozen mannequins had been posed all over the house: washing dishes at the fake sink, lying on the floor of the bedroom, looking out the window. Personally, Cordelia thought this was a lot creepier than any ghost, and got out of there as soon as possible. They texted Laurel, who told them that through a quirk in its construction, that particular house had proven to be unhauntable. They could just ignore it and move on.

They didn't ask her about the mannequins. Cordelia wasn't sure she wanted to know.

As their day wound down, and they were all getting tired and prickly, they came to another house that was noticeably different than the others. Instead of playing family memories, the life windows showed only classic films. Most were in black and white, many with subtitles. Quite a few were horror movies. Cordelia recognized some of the famous monsters, but the only movie she had actually seen was an old ghost story called *The Innocents*, which she had watched as research the previous summer.

They found the resident of the house upstairs.

He was glowing.

It was barely discernable, just a hazy nimbus of blue. Other than that, the ghost didn't look unusual. He was a pudgy man wearing a red sweater and thick glasses. The old movie that currently held his attention looked pretty spooky: a woman swimming in a pool while shadows danced along the wall and something growled in the background. The ghost watched intently and mimed writing in a notebook.

"He doesn't look like he's about to turn into a phantom," Benji said after Agnes had tapped the red circle on the map.

"The change probably happens without warning," Agnes said. She snapped her fingers. "Like that."

Benji took a step closer to the front door.

"Why didn't we ever see any of the Shadow School ghosts glow?" Cordelia asked.

"It takes decades for ghosts to turn into phantoms," Agnes said. "The ones at Shadow School never lasted that long. Either the ghost scavengers got them or we freed them. But this guy might have been haunting his house for a long time before Laurel brought him here. Check out all these black-and-white movies. Those were probably recent when he was alive."

Within minutes, they heard a car screech to a stop. Laurel and Kyle ran into the house with their equipment.

"Barry DeWitt!" Laurel exclaimed. Her face was flushed with excitement. "I wouldn't have picked him to turn so quickly. Big film buff, as you could probably tell. Reviewed movies for his local paper. He's definitely glowing?"

Cordelia nodded. "He doesn't look very dangerous, though."

"And now he never will be, thanks to you. Let's get him out of here."

Mr. Dewitt's attention remained riveted to the movie while Kyle and Agnes pieced together the ghost tent. In short order, the critic was safely sealed inside a boo-tube. His mist flickered like a film strip running through a projector.

"You guys did great today," Laurel said, slipping the boo-tube into its protective sleeve. "Why don't you head back early? Trish has your pay for today. I even threw in a little bonus for a job well done."

"Thanks!" Benji exclaimed.

With extra time on their hands, they decided to take a different route back to the office. Cordelia lagged behind her friends and thought about the day. She supposed she was doing something useful, but it was nowhere near as satisfying as sending ghosts into their Brights. And what was going to happen to poor Mr. DeWitt? Was he just going to stay frozen forever?

We could bring him to Shadow School, she thought. *Phantom or not, the dehaunter would send him along his way.*

It was a good idea. But she couldn't make it happen without telling Laurel the truth about their other life— which she wasn't willing to do without Dr. Roqueni's permission. Mr. Dewitt would have to wait for now.

They passed the purple house.

Cordelia slowed down for a better look. There was nothing particularly menacing about the house's appearance. The color was pretty, even peaceful, like the bouquets of dried lavender Cordelia's mom sometimes placed on their dining room table.

For a moment, Cordelia considered getting off her bike and peeking in a window. She was curious to see the terrifying phantom that seemed to frighten even Laurel.

"Come on, Cordelia!" Benji called back from the end of the street. "You're so slow!"

Cordelia took one last look at the house, then pedaled faster to catch up to her friends. For once, she had seen enough ghosts for the day.

11

Esmae

On a cold morning near the end of February, they pulled into the horseshoe driveway of a massive red mansion wearing a cap of snow. There were several packages on the front stoop.

"Does someone live here?" Agnes asked in surprise. They had visited over a dozen haunted houses in the past six weeks. Until now, all of them had been abandoned.

"The Connolly family," Laurel said. "Nice people. But they haven't stepped foot in the house since Wednesday. They refuse to come back until we've taken care of the ghost. I'll show you why."

Laurel pulled out her phone. While she swiped

and pecked—presumably searching for whatever she wanted to show them—Benji began to cough. He had been suffering from a sinus infection all week but was still adamant about coming to work today. His parents had begun to rely on his weekly pay, and he didn't want to let them down.

He's the best son in the world, and they don't even know it, Cordelia thought. She felt the sudden urge to give him a giant hug and maybe even a kiss. On the cheek. Probably.

Benji noticed that she was staring at him. "What?" he asked.

Cordelia handed him a tissue. "Your nose is running."

Laurel turned in her seat to face the kids. Her auburn hair had been tied into a tight bun that day, and it gave a severe pinch to her otherwise pretty features. "Our research team dug up a little more about this one than usual. Her name was Esmae Givens—"

"It still is," said Cordelia.

"—and she was only nine when she died. I won't get into details, but let's just say it was the kind of death that leaves an impression. She's not just a regular ghost. She's a phantom."

Between coughs, Benji said, "You told us we'd never have to . . . catch one of those," he managed.

"That was my intention," Laurel said, still searching through her phone. "But you're doing so much better than I expected. It's like you've been around ghosts for years! Besides, Esmae's not so bad for a phantom. Look."

She turned her phone so they could all see the screen.

It was one of those boring birthday videos that parents posted on social media and no one actually watched. A homemade banner attached to the wall proclaimed Happy 8th Birthday, Caroline! Friends and family in pointy hats sat around a dining room table as a cake was placed in front of the birthday girl.

Everyone sang. Caroline closed her eyes, presumably making a wish.

The candles went out.

Caroline turned to the boy next to her—same eyes, same nose, probably her older brother—and blamed him for blowing out the candles. The boy protested his innocence, but no one seemed to believe him. Caroline's mom came to the rescue and relit the candles. The whole routine started over again.

This time they only made it through a single "Happy birthday to you" before the candles blew out on their own.

The guests exchanged nervous glances. An older

man leaning against the wall started to clap his hands—
"Trick candles! Good one!"—but stopped immediately
when the mother gave a quick shake of her head. One of
Caroline's friends removed her birthday hat and placed
it neatly on the paper plate in front of her, as if hoping
not to be associated with the whole strange affair.

The mother lit a single candle. It blew out. She stub-
bornly lit it again—and the cake catapulted across the
room, slamming into the wall. A round layer of pink
icing hung suspended for a moment before beginning a
slow slide to the floor.

The video ended just as the screaming began.

"She's a poltergeist," Agnes said.

"No more, no less," said Laurel. "This is not Seamus
Gideon raising animals from the dead. This is a little girl
who's angry she's never going to have another birthday
party. Still, I want you to be more cautious than usual.
Locate Esmae, quickly and quietly, and show us where
she is. After that, get out of the house. Let the grown-
ups worry about the dangerous part."

Benji was struck by another coughing fit. Everyone
stared at him as he reached for a bottle of water.

"Quietly, huh?" Agnes asked.

Laurel frowned. "I think you need to sit this one
out, Benji."

"I'm"–cough, cough–"fine! I just"–cough, cough–"need"–cough–"a minute."

"I can do it without him," Cordelia said. "Don't worry. I'm sneaky."

Laurel tapped the back of the chair with her fingers, considering. "You sure you're not scared?"

"Please. In Shadow School I once saw this"–Benji's coughing suddenly got louder, warning Cordelia to watch her words–"giant rat in the cafeteria. *That* was scary. I can handle one little phantom."

With that settled, Cordelia slid out of the van and entered the house. The foyer had a cathedral ceiling with a glittering chandelier and a staircase branching off in two directions. A giant fish tank that looked like it had been stolen from an aquarium sat against the wall. The filter made a bubbling sound.

Cordelia walked into the dining room.

Caroline's birthday banner was still there, though the tape on the right side had peeled away, causing it to hang askew on the wall. Paper plates and overturned plastic cups littered the table. Someone had cleaned the cake off the wall, but they hadn't done a very good job. Sticky strings of icing clung to the wall like sweet worms.

Cordelia found a comfortable place on the couch

and slid the spectercles over her eyes. After the world finally stabilized, she rose to her feet—a little unsteadily at first—and searched the first and second floors. It took a long time. There were rooms within rooms and closets big enough to be studio apartments. Cordelia actually had trouble finding her way back to the foyer. She wondered if she should have brought bread crumbs.

There was no sign of Esmae.

With a sigh of resignation, Cordelia returned to the first-floor hallway and opened the door she had been saving until last, hoping she wouldn't need it. Wooden steps led down into a dimly lit basement.

"Of course you're down there," she muttered.

Cordelia descended. As she did, a series of thumping noises seemed to follow her down the stairs, echoing her footfalls. She tried not to think about it. The whole basement was basically a giant playroom. Toys, sleeping bags, and stuffed animals covered the floor. Apparently a sleepover had been part of Caroline's birthday plans. The few windows, set high in the walls, were covered by thick curtains, leaving barely enough light to see by. Cordelia nearly stepped on a board game that had been stopped in progress. The last person had rolled a four.

Cordelia navigated the minefield of toys and found Esmae staring at a shelf of dolls. For the most part, she looked like a regular nine-year-old girl. Her blond hair was short—except for the bangs, which covered her entire forehead—and her eyes were a pretty shade of blue.

A tiny flame flickered from each finger of her right hand, giving it the appearance of a candelabra.

Esmae held her hand out in order to illuminate the dolls, which she studied with disquieting intensity. Only four fingers of her other hand were lit. Cordelia remembered that Esmae had died when she was nine and wondered if there was a connection.

Keeping her eyes on the ghost, Cordelia slowly reached for her phone. She texted Laurel—found her downstairs—and watched as Esmae tried to pick up a plastic doll wearing an equestrian uniform. Her fingers passed right through it, leaving a trail of blue smoke. She stomped her feet in a ghostly tantrum and let loose with what surely would have been a doozy of a scream, had she been alive.

Cordelia took an instinctual step backward and knocked a tower of Jenga blocks to the floor.

Esmae extended her hands in Cordelia's direction, bathing her in a glow of otherworldly blue light. A smile stretched across her ghostly lips. She looked as though a friend had just come over for an unexpected playdate.

"Hi," Cordelia said with a hesitant wave.

Esmae blew out a single flame of her candled fingers.

The Jenga blocks rose into the air. Cordelia dove to the floor as they shot across the room, barely missing her. She looked up in time to see Esmae blow out a second flame, causing a tower of board games to topple in her direction. The corner of a wooden box stung her ankle.

She backed away from Esmae, who teasingly raised the flame of her index finger to her pursed lips—and then the world went blurry, as though someone had run their fingers across a wet painting and smeared all the colors together. *The spectercles*, Cordelia thought. *Not now*. She tried to find the exit but went the wrong way and heard the crunch of toys beneath her feet. Something hard rammed into her knee.

There was no time to wait for the blurriness to get better on its own. Cordelia removed the spectercles.

Her vision of the real world instantly cleared, but she could no longer see Esmae. Cordelia took two steps toward the basement stairs, and a leather couch flipped across the room, blocking her path. A TV bolted to the wall began shaking like crazy, eager to escape its moorings and take its shot at the intruder.

"Cordelia," Laurel whispered from the top of the stairs. "You down there?"

"Yes! Help!"

Laurel rushed down the stairs and shoved the couch out of the way. Kyle was right behind her. He began unpacking equipment, pausing to give the TV a nervous glance. It was shaking harder than ever.

"Where is she?" Laurel asked.

"I'm not sure."

"What's that supposed to mean?"

Cordelia shrieked. She had felt five tiny flames brush against the back of her neck.

"What's wrong?" Laurel asked.

"We should go."

"Not until we've done what we came here to do." Laurel extended the rod. The portable screen unfolded into place. "This job needs to be completed tonight."

"Why?"

"Just point me in the right direction. I'll take it from there."

At that moment, the TV broke free with an explosion of anchor screws and drywall dust. It shot across the room like a missile. Laurel ducked in time, but Kyle wasn't so lucky. The TV clipped him in the head before crash-landing in an overstuffed toy chest.

Kyle went down and didn't move.

"Kyle?" Cordelia asked. She started toward him, but Laurel grabbed her by the shoulders.

"Where's the phantom? Tell me!"

"I don't know!" Cordelia exclaimed. Tears stung her eyes. "I can't see her!"

Laurel shoved her away. "I'll do it myself!" she exclaimed, tapping her watch. An old commercial began playing on the screen. A smiling girl with pigtails whispered in a doll's ear while a voiceover narrator said, "Who's the only friend you can trust? Secret Sally!" Laurel swung the screen rod around the room, hoping to snag Esmae's attention.

Cordelia rushed over to Kyle. His eyes were open but dazed, and his left temple was matted with blood.

"Kyle's hurt," Cordelia said. "We have to go!"

"Not without the ghost!" Laurel hissed.

At that moment, Benji stumbled down the stairs, followed by Agnes. "Behind you!" he screamed to Laurel, who spun around and thrust the screen forward as though it were a crucifix warding off a vampire. The commercial changed. A girl pushed a doll on a swing while singing, "Playful Patty, Playful Patty . . ."

"You got her," Benji said. "She's totally hypnotized by that . . . extraordinarily creepy doll video." He coughed into his arm and then squinted. "Does that ghost have flames coming out of her fingers?"

Kyle touched his wounded head. "A TV hit me," he said.

"Are you okay?" Cordelia asked.

"I'll live. Let me set up this ghost tent so we can get out of here."

He tried to sit up. It didn't go well. Cordelia slid her coat beneath his head and helped him back down again.

"I'll get some ice," Benji called down.

"You rest," Agnes told Kyle, patting him gently on the shoulder. "I can set up the tent on my own."

"I'll help," said Cordelia, rising to her feet.

"No," Laurel said. Her cold eyes bored into Cordelia. "You wait upstairs. I think you've done quite enough for today."

12

The Legacy of Leland Knox

No one spoke during the return trip to Shady Rest. When they reached the main office, Kyle headed home, and Laurel told the kids to wait in the conference room while she took Esmae's boo-tube to the freezer. Cordelia felt like she had just been sent to the principal's office. She found a seat and put her head on the table.

"What happened in there, Cord?" Benji asked. His cough had gotten a lot better. Cordelia had found him some cold medicine in one of the medicine cabinets, along with a first-aid kit that Laurel had used to clean and bandage Kyle's wound.

"The spectercles glitched," Cordelia said. "I couldn't

even look through them without getting dizzy. I had to take them off."

Benji asked, "Like at the house with the toothpick ghost?"

"This was a lot worse—but same idea."

"This happened before?" Agnes asked. Cordelia couldn't tell if she was annoyed or concerned. Probably a little of both. "Why didn't you tell me?"

"It's already so lame that I need the spectercles to begin with," Cordelia said in a small voice. "And now they don't even work right? It's embarrassing."

"Were those the only two times the spectercles glitched?" Agnes asked.

"Yes. Except for all the other times."

"How many other times are we talking about?"

"Two. Maybe five. Probably twelve."

Benji and Agnes exchanged a harried look, like the parents of a particularly problematic child. "You should have told us," Benji said.

"It was never an issue before! We only dealt with nice ghosts! If I got a little dizzy every now and then, it wasn't a big deal. But today . . . ugh! I feel so bad. What happened to Kyle was my fault."

No one disagreed. They had been friends too long, and gone through too much, to give false words of consolation.

"He'll be okay" was all Agnes could offer.

They waited in silence. Laurel would return at any moment, and they didn't want to risk being overheard. Cordelia yawned. The horrors of Esmae's house had drained her, and she thought she could have easily sprawled out on the table and taken a nap.

After a few minutes, Agnes asked, "What's taking Laurel so long? The freezer's in the basement, isn't it?"

"For the regular ghosts," Cordelia said. "Maybe there's a different one for phantoms. I know I wouldn't keep them in the main office. What if there was a power outage?"

"Good point."

"How are we playing this when she gets back?" Benji asked. "Laurel's going to want to know why Cordelia freaked out. Should we tell her about the spectercles?"

"No way," Agnes said. "We'd have to tell her about Shadow School too. I still don't trust her enough for that."

Cordelia heard footsteps approaching the conference room. She resisted the urge to hide underneath the table.

"What do I say?" she asked.

Benji smiled. "You'll think of something. You always do."

Laurel entered the room and shut the door behind

her. There were quite a few open seats, but she chose to sit on the edge of the table instead. "Benji, Agnes. You mind leaving me and Cordelia alone for a minute?"

"Yes," said Agnes.

"Whatever you have to say to her, you can say to us too," added Benji.

"Fine," Laurel said. She was trying to play it cool, but Cordelia could tell their refusal to leave bugged her. "What happened?"

Cordelia could think of only one lie that fit. "I guess I just got scared."

"Scared? You said you couldn't even see the ghost."

"I panicked, okay? It was so dark down there. I could barely see!"

Laurel crossed her legs and gave Cordelia a dubious look. "You never struck me as the panicking sort. You've been around plenty of ghosts."

"Esmae wasn't a ghost. She was a phantom. And she was way scarier than Seamus Gideon."

Benji rolled right with it: "I was scared too. That girl was *freaky*."

Laurel seemed to find their explanation reasonable enough, even if she didn't look happy about it. "I appreciate your honesty, Cordelia, but what happened today is completely unacceptable. Kyle may need stitches. That's on you."

"I know," Cordelia said, looking down at the table.

"If you can't handle more intense hauntings, then maybe–"

Agnes rocketed from her seat and pointed an accusing finger at Laurel. "None of this is Cordelia's fault. It's *yours*. You're the one who sent a kid alone into a house with a dangerous phantom! Cordelia's lucky she's still alive!"

A range of emotions passed across Laurel's face. First, wide-eyed astonishment, then anger, and finally a sort of reluctant acceptance. Laurel nodded to herself, leaving Cordelia with the feeling that some sort of decision had been made.

"You're right," she said in a defeated voice. "I never should have sent you into that house alone. I was in a rush to capture Esmae, and it clouded my thinking. I'm sorry."

Laurel hopped down from the table and fell into the nearest seat. Cordelia and her friends exchanged uncertain looks. The conversation had taken an unexpected twist, and they didn't know how to proceed.

"Why the hurry?" Agnes asked. "We could have just come back another day."

Laurel poured herself a glass of water from a pitcher on the table. She took a long sip before speaking. "A while ago, I mentioned that we sometimes get paid to catch troublesome spirits. Esmae was one of those. The Connollys hired Shady Rest to get rid of her. And they're the type of people with more money than time, so they promised to pay twice as much if we could finish the job today."

"You risked Cordelia's life for *money*?" Agnes asked.

"I don't care about the money!" Laurel exclaimed, insulted by the implication. "I care about Shady Rest! The business needs more income if it's going to survive. I already let half the staff go, and I stopped building those fancy houses that Grandpa loved. From now on, every ghost gets the same dinky ranch."

"Like Mr. DeWitt's," Benji said.

"Yeah. Grandpa would roll over in his grave, but that's all we can afford. Which is why I need to charge for our services. If Shady Rest goes bankrupt, all those ghosts we've supposedly rescued are going to be at risk. Their haunts will either get sold or destroyed. I can't let that happen. Shady Rest is my grandfather's legacy. It's my responsibility to protect it."

"You really loved him," Cordelia said.

"Everyone loved him," Laurel said. "The man was a saint. But yes—me most of all." She sniffled and wiped her eyes. "Can I be honest? I worry about what he'd think, if he were here. Grandpa never accepted money for anything involving the ghosts. He viewed helping them as a moral responsibility."

"Why can't it be both?" Benji asked. "You can help people and still get paid. Besides, these Connolly people seemed like they could afford it."

He gave Cordelia a nervous glance, expecting an argument. She understood why. Given her past actions, it was a fair presumption that she would agree with Mr. Knox's view on "moral responsibility" and might have an issue with being paid for their services. Now that she knew the whole story, however, Cordelia found it hard to argue with Laurel's way of doing things. By capturing a phantom, Shady Rest was keeping homeowners safe from the dead. The money earned was then used to help the dead exist among the living. The entire system possessed an appealing balance.

"Since we're using the money to help the ghosts," Cordelia said, "I don't have an issue."

Benji looked pleasantly surprised. He might have even told her so, had his cough not chosen that moment to make a sudden reappearance.

"Thank you," Laurel said. "You kids are amazing. But now that you know the truth, I understand if you don't want to work here anymore. Helping ghosts is one thing. Capturing phantoms is another. They were too scary for Victor, and he was a grown man. That's why he left."

"You told us Victor quit because he was tired of the ghosts," Agnes said.

"Exactly. He was tired of them being so scary."

"That's not the same thing," Agnes said.

"Well, that's what happened. You know everything now. Promise."

Benji's phone dinged. He checked it and said, "My dad's waiting outside."

"See you next week," Laurel said. It was as much a question as a statement, and Cordelia thought she caught a hint of desperation in her voice. Laurel had already lost Victor. She couldn't risk losing them as well.

"I don't know," Benji said. "Ghosts are dangerous enough, but phantoms? My family could definitely use the money, but it's not worth getting killed over."

Laurel said, "I'll triple your pay."

Benji pumped his fist into the air. "Let's catch some phantoms!" he exclaimed.

"I'm in," Agnes said. "Cordelia?"

Her friends waited for her to agree, certain she would. After all, when had Cordelia ever turned down an opportunity to help the ghosts? They didn't understand that things were different now. A new fear had taken root in her mind, far more terrifying than the phantoms themselves: *What if my spectercles glitch again? It might not be Kyle who gets hurt next time. It might be Benji or Agnes.*

"I have to think about it," Cordelia said.

"I understand," Laurel said. "And I respect your decision, one way or the other."

There was no desperation in her tone this time. Indeed, she punctuated her last sentence with the slightest of shrugs, as though she didn't care one way or the other if she ever saw Cordelia again. After all, Benji had already agreed to return.

She only needed one of them.

That Monday, Cordelia had math first period. She met Benji at his locker so they could walk to class together. He looked a lot better, though his nose was still red.

"Hey, Rudolph," Cordelia said.

"Ha, ha," Benji said, closing his locker door. "Are you ready for this math test?"

"I have a sharpened pencil and feelings of anxiety. So . . . yes?"

Agnes took an accelerated math course on the other side of the school, so this was one of the few times that Cordelia and Benji walked to class alone. Normally their conversations were fluid and natural, but something had changed in the past few weeks. Silences were longer. Pauses more awkward.

"So, Saturday." Benji whistled. "That was crazy. I didn't see Esmae in full-fledged poltergeist mode like you did, but she still seemed pretty scary."

"Definitely not on my list of favorite ghosts."

"I'm sorry I didn't go in the house with you from the start."

"You were sick. And you did sort of save the day at the end. Why'd you decide to come inside anyway?"

"You had been in there forever. I was worried. I couldn't just not do anything. If something had happened to you, I never would have forgiven myself."

Cordelia knew she was blushing but met his eyes anyway. "Well, I'm glad you came. I'm sorry I didn't tell you about the spectercles sooner."

"That's okay. But next time I do something stupid, you can't get mad at me."

"Deal."

"Do you think Agnes could fix the spectercles? She created an entire dehaunter. This should be a snap."

"You would think. But according to Agnes, it's like night and day. The dehaunter involved math and science. The spectercles are basically magic. She wouldn't even know where to begin."

"Did they ever glitch when she was wearing them?"

"Nope. Agnes's theory is that the spectercles don't

have to work very hard in Shadow School, because the archimancy already makes it easier to see the ghosts. But when I'm out and about, it's a different story. It forces the spectercles to work a lot harder, and sometimes they–I don't know. What's the magical equivalent of blowing a fuse?"

"Glitching," Benji said. He gave her a quizzical look. "Do you really have a list of favorite ghosts?"

Cordelia counted them off with her fingers. "Mr. Derleth's son first. Obviously. Then the girl with the pointy hat and bow. Her Bright was this animated fantasy world with purple uni-cats, so I'm giving her extra points for originality. There are only so many tropical islands I can look at. I mean, it's your own personal heaven, people. Use your imagination! Third is a tie. The man playing the ukulele and–" She noticed the amused expression on Benji's face. "Sorry. I'm babbling."

"That's okay. It's funny. You don't talk about the Shady Rest ghosts the same way." He straightened his schoolbag. "Have you decided if you're coming back or not?"

"Not yet," Cordelia said. She had spent all Sunday thinking about it. On one hand, she was terrified of her spectercles going haywire at an inopportune moment. On the other hand, how could she just abandon her friends? What if one of them got hurt because she wasn't there to help them?

There was no good option. It was like a multiple-choice question where the teacher had forgotten to include the answer.

"Well, here's my take," Benji said. "I don't think the spectercles were the reason everything got screwed up. I think it was because we didn't go into the house together. If I had been there, I could have helped you. This whole ghost business has never been about just one of us. It's always been a team effort. You put the three of us together, and there's nothing we can't do. So along those lines, let me be brutally honest. I'm too scared to do this without you. You make me braver, Cordelia. Because I know if anything goes wrong, you'll figure out a way to save us in the end."

Cordelia studied her shoes. "That's sweet," she said, though it was infinitely more than that. *You make me braver.* It might have been the nicest thing anyone had ever said to her.

"Besides," Benji continued, "if you stopped coming every Saturday, think of how much you'd miss those ghosts of yours!"

"It's not the ghosts I'd miss," Cordelia blurted out. She saw Benji's look of surprise and quickly added, "You and Agnes. I'd miss both of you. My friends."

"Friends," Benji said, clearly disappointed. Being friends was nice. But it wasn't what he really wanted. He opened his mouth to say something else, and Cordelia's heart fluttered in her chest. *He's going to ask me out again,* she thought. *Right now.*

"What's the difference between a linear and nonlinear function?" he asked. "It was on the study guide, but I still don't get it."

She was surprised by how disappointed she was.

The Landmark Inn

Cordelia returned to Shady Rest the following Saturday.

Laurel seemed happy enough, but Kyle now regarded her with suspicion, as though at any moment she might lose her nerve and abandon him to the clutches of their invisible quarry. Cordelia hated the idea of anyone questioning her courage, particularly when it came to the ghosts, but there was no other way to explain her behavior without revealing her use of the spectercles. At any rate, Laurel seemed in no hurry to return to their ghost-hunting expeditions; except for a short trip to capture a "rose" about as frightening as the flower itself, the next few Saturdays were spent inspecting the village. They found, in total, two malfunctioning screens, one window that had broken in a recent storm, a hole in the wall that surrounded the property, and three glowing ghosts.

One afternoon, out of little more than boredom, they dared each other to see who could get closest to the purple house. Benji had managed to reach the front porch before he saw something dark sweep across the window.

It was the last time they played that game.

The snow melted, setting the stage for spring. Dr. Roqueni sent the kids a postcard from the Uffizi Gallery in Italy. Mr. Shadow had gone over to meet her, and they were having a wonderful time touring the sites together. That being said, she believed her "European adventure" was coming to a close. She missed the school, the students, and "even, if you'll believe it, the ghosts!"

Dr. Roqueni had already purchased her ticket for a return flight. She would be home in a month.

The kids were both excited and nervous. They had missed the principal, but she was going to be furious when they told her about Shady Rest (which they planned to do the moment they saw her, before they lost their nerve). Once things cooled down, however, Cordelia knew Dr. Roqueni would want to see the village for herself—which held the potential for some epic cross-over possibilities. For instance, right now phantoms and glowing ghosts had to remain frozen forever, with no hope of a happy afterlife. But if they opened their boo-tubes in Shadow School, there was a perfectly good dehaunter just waiting to set them all free.

Shadow School and Shady Rest, working together. The idea made Cordelia smile.

The week after Dr. Roqueni sent her postcard, things got crazy.

They hadn't gone on a single "phantom job" since Esmae's house, but that Saturday there were *three* paying customers in need of their services. The houses were relatively close to one another—two in the same town, amazingly enough—and Laurel hoped to capture all their phantoms in a single day. Normally Cordelia would be game for such a challenge, but she couldn't stop worrying about the spectercles. They hadn't glitched since Esmae's house, but they still made her nervous, like a dog that had bitten her once and could never be trusted again.

Fortunately, these new phantoms, while horrific in appearance, showed no inclination to harm them. The first one was the size of a small child, with insectile features and translucent nubs protruding from its shoulder blades like half-finished wings. The problem they faced with its capture was more practical than dangerous: the phantom sat on the edge of a bookshelf with its head cradled in its arms, and, as such, there was no way to get the ghost tent around it. After much deliberation, they decided to ease the bookcase from the wall. The phantom hovered in midair for a solid minute before drifting to the floor like a fallen leaf. From there it was easy pickings.

To find the next phantom, all they had to do was follow the trail of icicles that hung from the ceiling. These led them to the attic, where a screaming woman with flaming-red hair was encased in a block of ice like some sort of prehistoric discovery. Although unnerving, the phantom did not pose nearly as much threat as the attic floor, which was covered in a solid sheet of ice that made setting up the equipment a challenge. Every time Kyle fell, he glared at Cordelia as if it were her fault.

The last phantom was more pathetic than scary. His features were totally ordinary, except for the tiny blue handprints that had been pressed all over his face. As if this wasn't bad enough, he was trapped knee-high in the kitchen floor of his haunt, his bare feet dangling from the basement ceiling. His feet were covered with the same blue handprints. Cordelia imagined some ghost toddler tormenting him with finger paint while he was trapped.

They captured the ghost quickly. Cordelia thought he looked grateful.

As they left the house, the owner handed Laurel a white envelope. She slipped it into her pocket and gave the kids a smile of appreciation. Cordelia smiled back, feeling proud of herself. They had captured three phantoms in a single day. Best of all, her spectercles hadn't glitched once.

Things were looking up.

That Wednesday, they had an orientation at Cavendish Regional High School (which included students from Ludlow, Cavendish, and two other neighboring towns). Cordelia hated it. The building was new and modern, without any character at all, and the students seemed *too* happy, like they were hiding something. (Especially the pretty freshman who kept talking to Benji. Cordelia did not care for her *at all.*)

The other eighth graders wanted to stay at Cavendish all day, but Cordelia was glad when they finally returned to *her* school. As soon as the dismissal bell rang, she ran up to the mirror gallery to sketch the ghosts, which she hadn't done in months.

Agnes found her shortly afterward. She plopped

down on the floor and handed Cordelia a brown paper bag. "I forgot to give this to you this morning. It's a high-school-orientation brownie! I put sprinkles on top to represent all the new people we're going to meet."

Cordelia placed her drawing pad to the side and took a bite. The brownie was moist and delicious, but she didn't like the way the sprinkles got caught in her teeth.

Agnes said, "I just found out my friend Mark will be going to Cavendish too!"

"And we like Mark?"

"We do. But not how you're thinking."

"Ahh. What about the other one?"

"Kedar? He's going to some private school where you have to wear uniforms. Oh! They're finally showing that new anime in Denham. I've been dying to see it for months."

Cordelia vaguely remembered. "What was it called again?"

"*I Am Me, Are You?* Kedar asked if I wanted to go, but I don't want it to just be me and him. That's a little too datey. I was thinking you and Benji could come too. We could get ice cream afterward and try to figure out what the movie was about!"

"That's still datey. It's even worse. It's double datey. That's like . . . twice the datey."

"So what?" Agnes asked.

"So it might be awkward. Benji and I are just friends. Besides, he already asked me out once and I said no. I can't just change my mind."

"Why not?"

Cordelia didn't have a good answer. She had to admit that the idea of going to the movies sounded fun. (Maybe not the actual movie itself—the Benji part.) But then she thought about how out of place she had felt at Cavendish among the unfamiliar faces and ghostless halls.

Next year, she'd need Benji more than ever. She couldn't risk dating him and jeopardizing their friendship.

"Benji is just my friend," Cordelia said.

"Whatever you say," Agnes said, picking up the sketchbook and flipping through the pages. "Just me and you should go then."

"Sorry, Ag. You know I'm not a huge anime fan."

"But this one's four hours long!"

"Not a selling point."

Agnes flipped to the next page of the sketchbook. It was a drawing of a mean-looking girl in a white T-shirt and jeans. "Oh, I like this one! The artwork, I mean. Not the ghost. She's kind of scary."

"Thanks," Cordelia said. She was particularly proud

of the drawing, and gratified that someone else had noticed its quality was a notch above her others. "That's Esmae."

Agnes looked surprised. "Her dress and hair are pretty modern looking. You sure she was a phantom?"

"Very sure."

"That's weird, then. As far as we know, the only way to become a phantom is after jealousy for the living completely blackens your heart. That's a long process! In his journals, Elijah said it took at least seventy years, usually more. But Esmae looks like she could go to our school. How long can she possibly have been dead for? A few years? A decade?"

"Maybe she was already bad when she was alive. Gave her a head start on becoming a phantom."

"Elijah never mentioned it working like that, but I guess it makes sense. Or maybe he was just wrong about how long it took." Agnes closed the drawing pad and handed it to Cordelia. "It doesn't matter. The important thing is Esmae can't hurt anyone else."

"Exactly," Cordelia said.

The weather was beautiful that Saturday, and after their three-phantom marathon the previous week, Cordelia expected an easy day of work. Ideally, they wouldn't have to leave Shady Rest at all. She wanted to bike around the village with her friends, enjoying the sun.

As soon as Cordelia's mom dropped them off at the main office, however, Laurel led them straight to the van. "We'd better get started. Long drive today."

She wasn't kidding. They took the highway through Franconia Notch, where the Old Man of the Mountain used to watch passing travelers (Cordelia had learned about the famous outcropping during a far less eventful field trip), and rocketed past the breathtaking scenery that characterized northern New Hampshire. After crossing the Vermont state line, they exited the highway and passed through a cute town before turning at a fancy wooden sign reading The Landmark Inn and Convention Center. Kyle slowed down, in deference to the many speed bumps that lined the private road. To their left was a pond surrounded by a walking path, to their right a beautifully landscaped golf course. Given the ideal weather, Cordelia expected to see lots of people outside, but there wasn't a soul in sight.

At the end of the road sat a gigantic manor built from stones of varying hues. It looked like a castle. For some reason, Cordelia thought that might be important, though she couldn't figure out why.

The kids got out of the van and helped unload the equipment.

"If I told you how much it costs to stay at this place,

you wouldn't believe me," Laurel said. Cordelia liked her necklace today, a large emerald in an elegant setting.

"Maybe they should lower their prices," Benji said. "Business doesn't look so great."

"They had to close for the safety of their guests. The phantom was causing a ruckus."

"Like what?" Cordelia asked.

"Typical poltergeist activity. One woman had to go to the hospital to get stitches. And a few guests mentioned seeing strange shadows, though that might have just been their imaginations running wild. Either way, it's nothing we can't handle. Time is of the essence, though. The hotel is losing money every day they're closed."

Benji said, "I hope they're paying us well."

"Oh, believe me—they are," Laurel replied, looking very pleased with herself.

They entered a surprisingly modern lobby. Black-and-white photographs of the surrounding property were displayed on the walls, and freshly cut flowers had been tastefully arranged in clear vases. A man in his fifties stood behind the check-in counter. Cordelia had a feeling that she was catching him on a bad day. His suit was wrinkled, and his hair was sticking up every which way. Even his name tag sat slightly askew on his chest.

It read: Derek, Manager.

"We spoke on the phone," Laurel said. "My name is Laurel Knox. These are my associates."

Derek looked confused by the kids' presence. "Perhaps I wasn't sufficiently clear. This is an extremely dangerous situation."

Kyle laughed. "Don't worry about them."

"All you have to do is point us in the right direction," Laurel said. "We'll take it from there."

Derek still looked a little uneasy, but in the end his desire to have a ghost-free hotel trumped his concern for the children. "I don't know where she is now, but I can tell you where this entire thing started. There was a presentation in the Ellison Room—something to do with the future of real estate. I was standing right here when people started running up the stairs, screaming. At first I thought it was a fire or something. Then they told me what happened. In the middle of the presentation, chairs and objects started flying everywhere. It's a blessing no one was badly hurt."

"Definitely a poltergeist," Benji said.

"You called the ghost a 'she,'" Cordelia said. "How do you know? Did one of the guests see something?"

"Nothing like that," Derek said. "I just know our ghost. Everyone who works here does. Wendy has haunted the Landmark for forty years. Every so often a guest or staff member will catch a glimpse of her—especially when it snows. There was a huge blizzard the day she died." Derek's expression grew thoughtful. "She's never done anything like this before, though. Wendy's always been a rather nice ghost—almost like a mascot."

That was before she turned into a phantom, Cordelia thought.

"Don't worry, sir," Laurel said. "We'll have her out of here in no time flat. Now let's talk about our fee. . . ."

While Laurel spoke to Derek, and Kyle and Agnes did some last-minute checks on the equipment, Cordelia and Benji set off to find the ghost. The Ellison Room seemed a good place to start. They followed the signs to a part of the hotel with larger rooms intended for workshops and presentations. Delicate piano music piped through the speakers.

"Don't forget your spectercles," Benji said.

Cordelia slipped them on. There was barely any dizziness at all, which did little to reassure her. She suspected the spectercles were lulling her into a false sense of complacency so they could glitch again at the most inopportune moment.

"Do you think it's a little strange that Laurel and Kyle never come with us to find the ghosts?" Cordelia asked.

"Not really," Benji said. "We're like scouts. Once we find the enemy, we tell the troops where they are."

"It's hard for me to think of ghosts as the enemy," Cordelia said. "But I get what you mean. Still. It's almost like they're sending us ahead to make sure it isn't dangerous."

"It won't be. As long as we don't get too close."

They passed a long table with a red tablecloth. On it were three coffee tureens and picked-over platters of bagels, mini-muffins, and Danishes. The food was beginning to draw flies.

"Guess no one wanted to come clean up," Cordelia said. "Not that I blame them. How did Derek find Shady Rest's phone number to begin with? It's not like they advertise. When we first started, I tried to find them online and I—"

"Here it is," Benji said.

They reached a pair of double doors with a simple placard that read Ellison Room. One of the doors was slightly ajar. There was very little light coming through the crack.

"Ready?" Benji asked.

"Sure."

Benji opened the door, revealing a large room—practically an auditorium—with a projection screen hanging from the ceiling. The lights were off, and the curtains on either side of the room had been closed, allowing only a few weak beams of daylight to steal into the room. At one point, Cordelia suspected the folding chairs had been arranged in neat rows, but it looked as though a windstorm had breezed through them. A man sat in the only chair that hadn't been knocked to the floor. He didn't notice their entrance. His attention was completely focused on the blank screen in front of him.

"There he is," Benji whispered, already heading back out the door. "Let's tell Laurel."

"Wait. The manager said the ghost was a woman."

"Guess he was wrong."

"No way. She's been haunting this place for forty years, remember? Something's off here. You text Laurel. I'm going to take a closer look."

She crept across the room, stepping around the fallen chairs. The phantom didn't move. *That's definitely a man,* she thought, seeing him even more clearly now. *But how is that possible? Are there two ghosts?* Cordelia was hoping a glance at the phantom's face might help clear up the mystery. She knew it would be safer to wait for Laurel and Kyle to arrive, but her instincts were screaming that there was something important to discover here, if only she was brave enough to look.

She heard footsteps to her left and saw Benji taking a different path through the labyrinth of folding chairs, approaching the phantom from the opposite side. *He didn't leave me*, she thought. Benji gave her a nervous, adorable smile, and Cordelia was so distracted she nearly stumbled over a woman's pocketbook. Now that she was looking, she noticed other purses scattered between the chairs, along with abandoned coats, phones, and coffee cups. The last group had left in a hurry, and no one had been back since to retrieve their abandoned items.

The phantom was less than ten feet away now.

He was on the heavy side and wearing a red sweater and corduroy pants. There was something covering his eyes. It was too large to be glasses, but it had a circular shape. Cordelia would have to go past him and turn around in order to get the complete picture. Unfortunately, that meant putting herself in his line of sight for a single, horrifying moment, but there was no other way.

Cordelia took a few more steps, ready to turn and run at a moment's notice. *What is he wearing over his eyes?* She had to find out.

Just a few more steps. Quiet . . . quiet . . .

There was a loud clanging noise to her left, like someone hitting a locker. Benji mouthed the word, "Sorry."

When Cordelia looked back at the phantom, it was staring straight at her.

She screamed. Two film reels covered his eyes, as though his body had been fused with a small, ghastly projector. The reels began to spin. The phantom opened his mouth and light shone forth onto the screen. Within its twin beams a flickering tornado appeared, like something from an old black-and-white movie. It bounced around the confines of the screen, growing in both size and ferocity—and then it slipped into the real world and hovered before them. Although it still retained the two-dimensionality of its original form, the twister was clearly more than just a moving image. Cordelia could feel the wind on her face and hear the seats around her begin to rattle. The twister moved forward, and the first few rows of chairs were sucked into its vortex and spit out again in every direction.

"Cordelia!" Benji screamed, his voice nearly lost in the roar of the wind. He was already halfway to the exit and waving for her to follow. Cordelia leaped over a pile of chairs and ran in his direction, feeling the vortex tugging at her back, and was within fifteen feet of the open doors when she felt her feet leave the ground. For a moment, she was flying backward, and then she managed to grab on to a metal column. A plastic chair narrowly missed her head before being sucked into the spinning maelstrom of debris.

She hugged the column tighter, her feet dangling

toward the screen, and saw that the tornado was not the only cinematic haunting birthed by the strange phantom.

Walking in her direction, struggling only a little against the storm, was a shambling mummy. Like the tornado, it looked like a black-and-white movie come to life. She was sure it was real enough to hurt her, however. The stench of it was nearly unbearable, five thousand years spent festering in a tomb.

The mummy reached for her, its rotting fingers brushing the bottom of her sneakers. Cordelia kicked the creature's hand away but nearly lost her grip on the column in the process. She was slipping fast. Even worse, Cordelia saw the phantom's reel-eyes spinning again. A wolfman peeled itself off the screen, paused a moment to howl in celebration of its newfound freedom, and headed in her direction.

The mummy clutched her forearm.

The creature might have been little more than a moving image, but the strength of its grip was painfully real. It opened its mouth in a horrible smile, and an ancient worm squirmed between the nubs of its teeth. The mummy took a step forward so that its face was only inches from hers and exhaled a dusty breath.

There was nothing Cordelia could do. If she let go of the column to try and escape the mummy's clutches, the tornado would toss her across the room. If she kept holding on, the mummy would have her.

I have to take my chances, Cordelia thought, and started to relax her grip. She saw Benji still standing near the door, hair flapping in the wind but otherwise beyond its range, bending down like a runner at the start of a race. "No!" Cordelia exclaimed, knowing exactly what her crazy friend was planning to do—but it was too late. Benji sprang out of his crouch and sprinted full speed in her direction, arms pumping in perfect rhythm, and threw himself into the storm feetfirst, letting the wind carry him like a human bullet. He struck the mummy dead center, and its chest caved in like an empty box. It went flying backward into the wolfman—who gave an almost endearing yelp of surprise—and both monsters were sucked into the vortex of the tornado. The twister became a blur of fur and linen bandages as the phantom's creations fought for their right to exist, this storm within a storm causing the tornado to spin out of control and slam against the ceiling.

It exploded into a drizzle of black-and-white light that tingled Cordelia's skin.

She ran to Benji, who had been pulled halfway across the room, and helped him to his feet.

"That was amazing," Cordelia said, hugging him tight. "Thank you."

"I think it was mostly luck. But you're welcome."

Their faces were close. Cordelia pushed a strand of hair out of his eyes.

The exit doors slammed shut behind them.

They weren't out of it yet. While Cordelia and Benji had been distracted by the mummy (and each other), the phantom had continued to reel new creations into the world. They were everywhere now. The one who had shut the doors was a bald vampire with bat ears and long razor-like nails. From their right approached a pack of slow-moving zombies. Their makeup looked fake, like something from an old movie, but Cordelia didn't doubt their ability to tear the flesh from her bones. She backed away and nearly walked into a group of three unsmiling children with platinum-blond hair and glowing eyes.

The phantom turned in their direction and applauded. To him, it was just another movie.

Which gave Cordelia an idea.

She dashed across the room, pulling Benji behind her, and yanked open a curtain. Sunlight hit one of the zombies. It instantly became more difficult to see, like the screen of a phone on a sunny day, before fading away completely. Benji, catching on quick, joined her in opening every curtain they could find. The vampire, appropriately enough, vanished in the sudden onslaught of light. The creepy children were next, followed by a panther they hadn't even noticed until then.

Cordelia ran to the front of the room and turned on the overhead lights. The phantom spun its reels in fury, trying to create some new horror, but nothing appeared. Now that the lights were on, it was too bright to see any images projected on the screen.

Benji and Cordelia heard the doors open behind them. Laurel, Kyle, and Agnes entered the room.

"What's taking you guys so long?" Laurel asked. "Did you find the phantom yet?"

Cordelia bit back a less than friendly retort and pointed out the phantom's location. He looked too disheartened to try to escape, and Cordelia was certain that capturing him, from this point, would be a breeze. While the other three set up the ghost tent, Cordelia and Benji headed back toward the lobby. There had been a pitcher of complimentary cucumber water on the counter, and Cordelia planned to drink half of it.

As they passed along a narrow hallway filled with guest rooms, Cordelia noticed that one of the doors was slightly ajar. It had not been open before. She peeked inside and saw a woman straightening the bed—or, at least, miming the movements. Her hands passed right through the pillow she was attempting to fluff.

"Benji," Cordelia whispered.

"I see her," he said.

The ghost was wearing a rust-orange uniform that said Landmark Inn. Her name tag said Wendy. She glanced in their direction with an apologetic look, as if this was their room and she didn't want her presence to disturb their stay. Cordelia and Benji parted to allow her to pass, then watched as she walked straight through the door of the next room.

"There are two ghosts haunting this place," Cordelia said.

"I guess."

It was only late that night, as Cordelia hovered somewhere between sleeping and waking, that all the pieces fell into place. The phantom's obsession with movies. His red sweater. The two ghosts. Why Laurel's employee had been so excited to show her "the castle."

Cordelia sat up in bed, instantly and totally awake.

"Oh no," she said.

14

Ice Cream and Revelations

There was too much to explain over the phone, so Cordelia arranged a meeting at Moose Scoops, Ludlow's local ice cream shop. In an attempt to stay profitable during the winter, the owner had purchased a couple of fancy coffee machines. It seemed to be working. The shop was crowded, mostly with teenagers As usual, Sawyer was working the counter. He was a young man who always had a dumbfounded expression on his face, as though you had just told him a joke and he was still trying to figure out the punch line. Cordelia liked him. He never rushed them out, no matter how long they lingered at their table, and even tossed them a free scoop of ice cream now and then.

"Hey, Sawyer," Cordelia said, approaching the counter while Benji and Agnes snagged a table. "How's it going?"

"It's going," Sawyer said. "What can I get for you?"

Cordelia ordered a decaffeinated cappuccino for herself, a scoop of ice cream for Agnes, and the mocha smoothie that Benji liked. After collecting their drinks, she joined her friends at the only available table. It wasn't as private as Cordelia would have preferred, but she doubted it mattered. The nearby teenagers were too involved in their own dramas to bother eavesdropping on a bunch of kids.

"How much do I owe you?" Benji asked, digging in his pocket.

"My treat," Cordelia said. She had a funny feeling that their working days might be over, and she didn't want Benji to waste his money. Perhaps he had already drawn the same conclusion, because instead of insisting he pay—as he normally did—Benji simply smiled and said, "Thank you."

Agnes hadn't even taken a bite of her ice cream, which was very un-Agnes-like. Cordelia could sense her moods in a way only a best friend could, and she had known within seconds that something was wrong.

It was possible, of course, that Agnes had come to the same conclusions as Cordelia—but if so, she would be angry, not sad.

This was something else. Something personal.

"You okay?" Cordelia asked.

"Not really," Agnes said. "But I want to hear what you have to say first. It's all part of the same big mess."

"Okay," Cordelia said. She pulled out her phone and opened the Notes app. "I couldn't sleep last night because of all the ideas bouncing around my head, so I decided to write them all down. I split my thoughts into three sections: Things We've Been Told, Things That Seem Wonky, and Next Steps. That last one is blank for now. I was thinking we could do it together."

"Wonky?" Benji asked.

"Let's start with Things We've Been Told," Cordelia said, checking her notes. "Shady Rest was founded by Leland Knox. He rescued endangered ghosts and moved them to safe locations. When Mr. Knox died, his granddaughter Laurel took over the business. Unfortunately, he didn't leave her enough money, so she was forced to take paying jobs capturing dangerous phantoms. When this proved too much for Victor—the only one at Shady Rest who could see the ghosts—he quit. Luckily, Laurel was hired by Gideon's Ark to rid them of their phantom, and that's where she met us."

Agnes made a soft *oomph* sound. Her uneaten ice cream was beginning to melt.

Cordelia squeezed her hand and continued. "Since Benji and I can see the ghosts, we replaced Victor. We have three major jobs. Locate at-risk spirits so Laurel can set them up in new digs. Keep an eye on the residents to make sure none of them are about to turn into phantoms. And, more recently, help Laurel and Kyle capture any phantoms causing trouble out in the world." Cordelia looked up from her phone. "That's the end of the first list. Did I leave anything out?"

"Sounds about right," Benji said.

"Okay," Cordelia said. "And now: Things That Seem Wonky. Let's start with the big one. I recognized the phantom we captured yesterday. His name is Barry DeWitt. Up until a month ago, he lived in one of the Shady Rest houses. All his life windows were old movies."

"I remember him," Benji said. "The movies are definitely a link, but how can you be sure—"

"The red sweater he was wearing. It stayed the same, even after he became a phantom. We told Laurel he was glowing, so his boo-tube should be chilling in the storage unit—yet somehow he ended up at the Landmark Inn."

"Could he have died there?" Benji asked. "Maybe his ghost somehow returned to its original haunt when it was frozen? It doesn't make a lot of sense, but . . ."

"I wondered the same thing, so I did a little research last night. Barry DeWitt died at his home in Massachusetts while watching some movie called *The Cabinet of Dr. Caligari*. It was in his obituary. The only person who ever died at the Landmark Inn was Wendy Jenkins in 1972."

"The maid," Benji said.

"We'll get back to her," Cordelia said. "She was, in a way, the reason we ended up there to begin with. But more importantly, there's no good reason why Mr. DeWitt should have been haunting the Landmark. Which leaves only one possible conclusion."

Cordelia stared into her cappuccino, not wanting to say the words out loud. Perhaps working for Shady Rest wasn't as satisfying as sending ghosts into their Brights, but it was *something*. She didn't want it to end.

"Laurel and Kyle moved Mr. DeWitt from Shady Rest to the Landmark Inn," she finally said. "On purpose."

There it was. Agnes and Benji gave reluctant nods. They didn't want it to be true, but there was no use pretending otherwise. The trio sat in silence, pondering the implications. A bell dinged as some kids from Shadow School entered the ice cream shop. Cordelia didn't know their names, but she had seen them around. They looked as if they didn't have a care in the world.

"I just thought of something," Benji said. "Cordelia–do you remember that clanging noise yesterday, the one that made Mr. DeWitt turn around?"

"It nearly gave me a heart attack! What was that, anyway?"

"I accidentally kicked something across the floor. I thought it was one of those metal water bottles, but now I'm not so sure. It was really heavy. It actually left a bruise on my big toe. Now I'm wondering if it might have been a boo-tube. Laurel and Kyle could have just hidden it in the conference room. By the time it thawed out and Mr. DeWitt broke free, they would have been long gone. Then when they got the call asking for help, they could have pretended they had no idea what was going on."

"And the Landmark would pay them to remove the phantom they left in the first place." Cordelia grimaced in disgust. "What a rotten thing to do. Like an exterminator sneaking a rat into a house, then charging the owner to get rid of it. They could have at least left a *nice* ghost so no one would get hurt."

"That wouldn't do the trick," Benji said. "It might just sit in the corner and watch the world go by. But a phantom–that's big and dramatic. Even people without the Sight notice those. They'd pay anything to get rid of it."

"It's not just Mr. DeWitt," Agnes said. "I did a lot of

research last night too. Esmae died three hundred miles away from the house we found her in. There was no reason for her to be there. She was probably a resident of Shady Rest at some point, just like Mr. DeWitt."

"Until Laurel and Kyle moved her," Benji said.

"They must have planted all the phantoms we helped capture," Agnes said. "The only thing I can't figure out is the archimancy factor. Not all houses are hauntable. How do they know which ones to pick?"

"I know the answer to that," Cordelia said. "When we first started at Shady Rest, I overheard Laurel talking to one of the office people." She struggled to remember his name. "Salesman type, strong cologne?"

"Carl," Agnes said with distaste.

Cordelia nodded. "He was showing her the Landmark Inn on a tablet and talking about how excited he was that a maid had died there and was haunting the place. That's the ghost Benji and I saw on the way out— Wendy. Which is how Laurel knew the Landmark was hauntable. It was already haunted. My guess is Carl's job is tracking down properties like that."

"Do you think the entire staff knows?" Benji asked.

"Probably," Agnes said. "Remember that one day when Laurel said she had a meeting about potential sites? I bet you they were planning which houses to put phantoms in."

"The bigger, the better," Benji added. "Rich people can pay more."

"Duh," Cordelia said, feeling stupid. The size of the houses, and the wealth of the families who owned them, should have alerted her that something was amiss. It seemed painfully obvious now. The whole complicated mystery was like a jigsaw puzzle. The more pieces they snapped into place, the easier it became to find where others belonged.

Benji laughed. "Sorry. I know planting phantoms inside someone's house is evil and all—but you have to admit, it's also kind of brilliant. I wonder how much she charges to—"

The girls stared at him.

Benji cleared his throat. "That's not important."

"There're still a lot of things I don't understand," Cordelia said. "Like how are they sneaking the boo-tubes inside these places? The Landmark's easy enough, but you can't just walk inside someone's house. And how do these owners know how to contact Shady Rest?"

Agnes and Benji didn't have any answers. Cordelia looked down at her empty cup and considered getting another cappuccino. Maybe with caffeine this time.

"There's still a lot to figure out," Benji said. "But I think we can safely say that if Laurel and Kyle keep leaving their phantom bombs all over the place, it's only a matter of time before someone gets killed. We have to stop them."

"How, though?" Agnes asked. "We can't go to the police. They'll never believe us."

"We need Dr. Roqueni," Benji said. "She'll know what to—"

"We can't tell her!" Agnes exclaimed, suddenly near tears. "It's too risky!"

Cordelia put her arm around Agnes's shoulders. "What's going on?"

"When I was trying to dig up information on Shady Rest last night, I found this video about Leland Knox. It answered a big question I had from the start." She dug her phone out of her pocket. "I'll show you. But I'm warning you now—it's going to hurt."

Cordelia, unsure how anything involving Shady Rest could elicit such an emotional reaction, was suddenly afraid. She watched the screen. It was a news story about "local philanthropist Leland Knox." After the anchorwoman gave the setup, there were a few interviews with people dressed in black standing just outside an impressive cathedral. They all seemed genuinely distraught that Leland Knox was dead.

When the clip ended, Cordelia and Benji stared at Agnes in confusion.

"What am I missing?" Cordelia asked.

"These interviews were shot the day of Mr. Knox's funeral. Let me find the right spot . . . now look carefully."

The screen had been paused. Cordelia didn't notice anything unusual about the woman being interviewed, so she looked past her, where several mourners were exiting the church. One man was in the process of putting on his fedora.

It was Darius Shadow.

"Oh man," Benji said. "Oh, Mr. Shadow. Not you . . ."

"So he's at the funeral," Cordelia said with a defensive shrug. "What does that prove? Mr. Shadow and Mr. Knox knew each other? Weird coincidence, sure, but it kind of makes sense. They're both old and they both love ghosts. Their paths must have crossed at some point. It doesn't mean they were best friends or anything."

Except Cordelia remembered now. The previous summer, Mr. Shadow had been really sad for a solid week or two. When Cordelia asked what was wrong, he had told her that his "very dear friend" had died. She recalled the phrase exactly because she had found it so touching.

"You're right, Cord," Benji said. "They're both obsessed with ghosts. That's probably how they became friends in the first place. Which means Mr. Knox definitely would have told Mr. Shadow about Shady Rest."

"So what if he did?" asked Cordelia. "Mr. Knox didn't know what his granddaughter was doing. That means Mr. Shadow didn't either."

"I want to believe that," Agnes said. "But if we accept that Mr. Shadow might be involved in all this—"

"No!" Cordelia exclaimed.

"—a lot of pieces start to click together. I always said it was really weird that Laurel and Kyle suddenly showed up at Gideon's Ark. But let's say Mr. Shadow told them that you and Benji had the Sight? All of a sudden it makes sense. They knew you were going to be there, so they left Gideon's boo-tube. That gave them a chance to come to the rescue so we could see what good people they were. Mr. Shadow knew that would win us over."

"He could have just introduced us."

"Not without revealing his involvement. Also, Dr. Roqueni's trip was his idea, remember? What if that was to get her out of the way? She was bound to get involved if she was here. And if something went wrong—as it has—she wouldn't be able to help us. We'd be on our own."

Cordelia refused to believe it. Mr. Shadow had sent Dr. Roqueni on her long-delayed European vacation as an act of redemption. This new version of events, which cast him as a villain with no desire to make amends with his niece, couldn't be right. It was too heartbreaking.

"Sorry, but I don't buy it," Benji said. Cordelia smiled with relief, glad it wasn't just her. "This is *Mr. Shadow* we're talking about. He's our friend. He wouldn't just betray us like this."

"I know," Agnes said. "But we've only known him a year. Dr. Roqueni has known him her entire life, and think about how much she's struggled to trust him. What if she was right and we were wrong? We have to at least consider the possibility. Right?"

"I guess," Cordelia mumbled. Although her heart told her otherwise, the evidence was hard to ignore.

"So you see why we can't ask Dr. Roqueni for help. She's in Rome right now with Mr. Shadow. If we tell her we're in trouble and she rushes home—Mr. Shadow is going to know something's up and warn Laurel that we know the truth."

Benji sighed. "Fine. I still don't think it's true, but I'm all for being cautious. We'll tell Dr. Roqueni when she gets home—when Mr. Shadow isn't around. But what do we do until then?"

"Nothing," Cordelia said. "If we stopped going to Shady Rest every Saturday, that would look really suspicious. Besides, what if Laurel sets another phantom loose? Who's going to stop it from hurting anyone?"

"So just play stupid and act like nothing's different?"

Benji said. "I can do that."

"That's not all," Cordelia said. "I think we should find Victor. Laurel said he quit because he was scared of the phantoms, but that's always seemed a little iffy to me. This guy has the Sight—the real kind, like Benji. I don't see him getting scared so easily. I bet he found out what was really going on and wanted no part of it. He might be able to help us."

"I love that idea," Agnes said, sipping the soupy remains of her ice cream. She seemed a little happier now that she had shared her burden with her friends. "How do we find him, though? We don't even know his last name."

"Leave that to me," Cordelia said.

As soon as she got home, Cordelia made a cup of milk tea, opened her Chromebook, and got to work. She loved tracking down information online—and she was good at it too. Her secret was faith. No matter how little Cordelia had to go on, she always believed that the information she needed was out there, waiting to be found. All it took was persistence—which she had in spades—and a little luck.

"Okay, Victor," Cordelia said, wiggling her fingers. "Let's see where you're at."

A last name would have been extremely helpful, but

Cordelia also looked forward to the challenge of finding an address or phone number without one. She started out with the keywords "Victor" and "New Hampshire," which gave her far too many results, then threw "Shady Rest" into the mix. That wasn't any help. Since the company had never demonstrated an online presence in the past, Cordelia wasn't surprised.

This, however, was a clue in itself.

Victor never could have found Shady Rest on his own, she thought. *Which means they must have found him instead.*

If Laurel had been looking for someone with the Sight, how would she have done it? Cordelia tried various combinations of "ghost," "ghost hunter," "psychic," "ghost expert," and "can see ghosts." In every instance, there were too many search results. After some thought, Cordelia realized that Laurel would have needed someone local, so she included "New Hampshire" and some nearby states. This reduced the number of results but didn't give her any useful information. She tried the same keywords but added "Victor" this time. For a moment, Cordelia thought she had something—a Vic Hayder of Massachusetts, whose cheaply made website promised a "glimpse into the ghostly void"—but she knew within moments that his proposed skills were just a hoax.

She decided to try a different approach.

When Victor had been hired, Leland Knox had still

been alive. If he was anything like Cordelia's grand-parents, he might not have been a huge fan of the internet. Instead, he'd have wanted to meet any potential employees in person. Only by looking them in the eye could he gauge whether they were the real deal and not a charlatan like Vic Hayder of Massachusetts.

But where could you meet someone with the Sight?

"Conventions!" Cordelia exclaimed.

She typed "Leland Knox paranormal convention" into the search bar. The first result was the lead she'd been looking for: *New Hampshire Spirit Expo*. It had been held in a Ramada Inn in Concord nearly three years ago, which fit the time frame for when Victor had begun working for Shady Rest. Mr. Knox himself had run a workshop entitled "Seeing Ghosts Is a Blessing, Not a Curse!" There was no list of students or photos of the workshop on the webpage, so Cordelia jumped to the convention's Facebook account and scrolled down . . . and down . . . and down . . . until she finally saw Mr. Knox. Just like all the other photos she had seen of him, he was wearing a bow tie and smiling like someone at total peace with the world. There was a small group of adults listening to his talk, but the photographer had been standing behind them, and she couldn't see their faces.

She glanced at the comments on the photo.

Ghostmama42: Enjoyed the talk. Nice man. Offered to "test" people who said they can really see the spirits but I think that part's a scam.

VicPrice: Not a scam.

Ghostmama42: For real? Did he test you?

VicPrice: ☺

"Hey, Victor Price!" Cordelia said, grinning with satisfaction. "It's nice to finally meet you."

Now that she had a last name to work with, it was only a matter of time before she found his contact information. She started with his Facebook page. Victor was sitting on a boulder in his profile pic, making her think that it had been taken on some sort of hike. He was in his thirties with round glasses and long brown hair tied in a ponytail. His account was restricted to friends only, so Cordelia couldn't access any additional photos, but it did reveal his place of residence as Brattleboro, Vermont. Cordelia reopened her search engine, combined this new information with Victor's first and last name, and pressed Enter.

The first search result was a newspaper article. She read the headline and her entire body went cold.

15

Cordelia and Benji Follow a Dot

H e's *missing?*" Benji asked.

His voice rose above the din of Monday-morning chatter as students made their way to class. Cordelia expected heads to turn in their direction, but no one seemed to care. They were too busy catching up with their own weekend gossip, which revolved more around scandalous texts and "totally unfair" homework assignments than potential crimes. Cordelia chuckled to herself. In comparison to what was going on at Shady Rest, life at her haunted school seemed almost normal.

"His mother reported him missing two months ago," Cordelia said, "though I get the impression the police aren't too concerned. This isn't the first time Victor has vanished. He once went to Argentina for three weeks on some sort of 'meditation hike' without telling anyone."

"I guess after he quit Shady Rest he could have just gone and started somewhere new," Benji said. "But it seems weird he wouldn't tell his mom."

"Maybe they didn't get along," Agnes said.

"She cared enough to call the police," Cordelia said. "Listen, I'll say what we're all thinking. Laurel and Kyle killed Victor and hid the body."

"I wasn't thinking that!" Benji exclaimed. He turned to Agnes. "Were you thinking that?"

"A little. We have to at least consider it. Victor quit Shady Rest and then vanished. Laurel must have been pretty mad that he refused to help her. It totally messed up her plans."

"So she *killed* him?" Benji asked in disbelief.

"Maybe he threatened to go to the police."

"So? No one would believe him. I agree that Laurel is doing some bad stuff, but there's a big difference between planting phantoms and cold-blooded murder."

"Why didn't Laurel tell us that Victor was missing, then?" Cordelia asked.

"Why would she know?" Benji asked. "He quit working for her. It would have been weird if she kept track of him afterward."

"True," Cordelia said, more confused than ever. When she had first read about Victor's disappearance, she had been certain there was some sort of foul play involved. Now she wasn't so sure. Victor was a grown man, and—as far as she could tell—a bit of a free spirit. He might have just wandered off.

"We need to get some adults involved," Agnes said. "Ghosts are one thing. But this is scary in a whole different way. I don't like it."

"We've been through this already," Cordelia said. "We can't go to the police or Dr. Roqueni. Not until she gets back, at least."

"Mr. Derleth, then," Agnes said. "Or—here's a crazy thought—our *parents*! I know we'll get in trouble for lying to them about our 'community service' at Shady Rest, but I'd rather get grounded than killed. We could have them wear the spectercles inside Shadow School. Once they see the ghosts for themselves, they'll know we're telling the truth."

"What is getting our parents involved going to accomplish?" Benji asked. "The police aren't going to take them any more seriously than they'd take us."

Benji was right. The kids were the only ones who could solve this problem. When it came to ghosts, their parents were the children, while they were the ones with knowledge and experience.

"So what do we do?" Agnes asked.

"Same thing as before," Cordelia said. "Act stupid and wait it out. When Dr. Roqueni gets back, we'll come up with a real plan."

"Okay," Agnes said. "But there is *one* thing I want to check out while we wait."

"I hate this idea already," Benji said.

"It might be nothing. But after what happened with Esmae, I've been paying attention to what Laurel does with the boo-tubes, and there is definitely a second freezer where she stores the phantoms."

"They're too dangerous to keep in the main office," Benji said with a shrug. "The second freezer must be in one of the empty houses."

"Then how come we've never seen it before? We've searched that village from top to bottom. Where's the freezer?"

"That is a little weird," Cordelia said.

"I even casually mentioned it to Laurel one time. You wouldn't believe how quickly she changed the subject. There's something she doesn't want us to know. I'm sure of it."

Cordelia was down for a little detective work—at least it would give them something to do until Dr. Roqueni returned. "Do you have a plan?"

"Not yet."

"What happened to lying low?" Benji asked. "If we get caught snooping around, Laurel will definitely know we're onto her."

"Good point," Cordelia said. "Let's make that step one of our plan: Don't get caught."

By Saturday, they were ready to find the second freezer.

If Laurel decided to take them ghost catching, their search would have to wait. Fortunately, it was an inspection day. Agnes had taken care of all the technical details, but in order for their plan to work, they still needed one more thing that was beyond their control. They didn't find it until two hours after their rounds began, when they entered Dr. Gill's house. The ghost wasn't in front of her wedding video today. Instead, she was watching a serious-looking man deliver a lecture entitled "Breakthroughs in Dentoalveolar Surgery" from behind a podium.

She was glowing.

"Finally," Cordelia said.

Agnes pressed the red circle on the tablet. Laurel and Kyle arrived within minutes. They were all smiles, which wasn't unusual when the kids found a potential phantom. It was the same way a foreman might react when a miner found a rare jewel embedded in the wall of a cave.

Laurel and Kyle were con artists—and maybe even

murderers—but they were good at their job. In no time at all, Dr. Gill was inside the boo-tube. The ghost's mist was the white of a freshly polished tooth. Since Laurel couldn't see the mist, Cordelia supposed they could have faked this part and used a regular ghost, but she wanted to be as cautious as possible.

"Good work," Laurel said. "That's one less phantom to worry about!"

Cordelia forced a smile to her lips. It was like pushing open a gate with rusted hinges. "Thanks," she said.

"Do you mind if I ride back with you?" Agnes asked. "I have to use the bathroom." She dropped her voice to a whisper, as though she didn't want Benji to hear—a nice touch. "I'd bike back, but it's sort of an emergency."

This wasn't such an odd request. The only functional bathroom in the entire village was in the main office. If Laurel and Kyle had been storing the boo-tube in the freezer for regular ghosts, bringing Agnes along would have been the easiest thing in the world. And yet there was no mistaking the look of annoyance that passed between them.

That's because they're not going back to the main office, Cordelia thought. *They're bringing the boo-tube to the secret freezer.*

Laurel hesitated before speaking, but she was stuck—there wasn't any feasible excuse to deny Agnes a ride.

"Of course," Laurel said. "Can you do me a solid, though, and catch up with Benji and Cordelia on your own afterward? Kyle and I have an errand."

"No problem," Agnes said. "I'm sorry to bother you."

"Don't be silly."

The moment they drove off, Cordelia took out her phone and tapped on Agnes's name in her contacts list. A map appeared on the screen, allowing her to see Agnes's location. Cordelia zoomed in as close as it would go and saw a red dot going down Redwood Lane—the main road that stretched from one end of Shady Rest to the other.

"It's working!" Benji exclaimed.

"As long as they don't see Agnes 'accidentally' leave her phone in the car," Cordelia said.

The dot stopped before a gray square that Cordelia assumed was the main office and remained there just long enough for Agnes to get out of the car. The phone, as planned, must have remained in the back seat, because the dot continued back along Redwood before making a left and heading across the development.

"Go, go, go!" Benji exclaimed, pushing Cordelia out the door. They hopped on their bikes and pedaled hard in the direction of the car, Cordelia bracing the phone against her handlebars so she could follow the dot's progress on the map. They could have just waited to see where the dot stopped and gone there after the car left, but Cordelia wanted to see what Laurel and Kyle were up to with her own eyes.

The red dot came to a halt.

Cordelia and Benji got as close as they dared and hid their bicycles. The location of the dot was just past the house in front of them, a majestic Victorian that had clearly been built when Mr. Knox was still alive. Going around to the front seemed risky, as there were no bushes or fences to conceal their presence, so instead they entered the Victorian through the back door and peeked out one of the front windows.

Laurel's car was parked outside one of the nondescript white ranches on the edge of the village.

"What are they doing in there?" Benji asked.

"I have no idea. We've been in that house before. There's nothing inside except a bunch of creepy mannequins. Laurel said they messed up the construction and it's not even hauntable."

"Or maybe she just said that so we'd skip it when doing our inspections. Pretty good way to keep us from looking too hard, right?"

Cordelia texted Agnes to let her know their location and settled in to wait, kneeling on the floor so only the top of her head would be visible through the window.

Within minutes, Laurel and Kyle exited the house. Cordelia couldn't hear what they were talking about, but Laurel seemed to be yelling at Kyle about something. He threw his hands in the air and shook his head, as though protesting his innocence, but Laurel wasn't having any of it. She no longer had the boo-tube. That meant it was either in the car (doubtful), at the main office (possible), or in the house.

Just before Kyle slid behind the wheel, he gave a glance in their general direction, perhaps just taking in the fine spring day. Both kids ducked beneath the windowsill. Cordelia stared at the front door, her heart bursting at its seams, sure that Kyle was going to barrel through it at any moment.

Instead, they heard the *vroom* of the motor as the car rocketed past the house. (There was no need for a speed limit in the village of the dead.) After waiting a few extra beats, they walked across the street and entered the house, acting as naturally as possible, on the off chance that someone saw them, they could always claim they were doing their jobs. Someone had moved the mannequins around since the last time they had been there. Three of them—an adult and two children dressed in casual clothes—sat at a makeshift table. The mannequins could bend at the hips, but not the knees, and their legs stuck straight out in a strange perversion of sitting. Someone had fanned out five playing cards in front of each of them and placed a pile of chips in the center of the table.

"Wow," Benji said. "And I thought ghosts were creepy."

"Look," Cordelia said, pointing at the floor. There was a trail of dirt leading through the living room. "My mom would kill me if I ever tracked dirt through the house like that. That's why I always leave my shoes at the door."

"Same here," Benji said. "Except my mom would make me sweep it up first. Then she'd kill me."

They followed the trail to the basement door. It was open. Cordelia could see dirt on the steps, though not as much as there had been in the living room: Kyle and Laurel had effectively used the entire first floor as their welcome mat, stamping dirt out of their treads a little bit at a time.

They started down the stairs.

"How is your mother, anyway?" Cordelia asked, making conversation to break the unnerving silence.

"Better," Benji said. "She just got promoted to assistant manager at the restaurant. My dad is making things happen too. He's a licensed electrician, so he's been doing odd jobs here and there. At first it was just people he knew, but word got out about how good he is, and now he's getting calls from total strangers. He's even thinking of starting his own business."

"Awesome," Cordelia said.

The basement was sparsely furnished with lawn furniture and two cardboard boxes labeled Washer and Dryer. Cordelia was relieved to see that there were no mannequins. Plastic faces in a dark basement was not what she needed right now. It would have been all too easy to imagine one turning in her direction.

They split up to take a look around.

"Things are definitely looking up, but money is still tight," Benji said. "It doesn't help that Sofia needs braces. I told my parents they should just let it go. So what if her teeth are a little crooked? It adds character. But Sofia wants to be an actress when she grows up. Perfect teeth are sort of a must."

Cordelia noticed a stained canvas drop cloth on the floor. It looked suspicious.

"Sofia's a good actress," Cordelia said. She had been to a few of her plays. "She might even be great when she's older. She can sing too."

"I guess," Benji said, who was far prouder of his sister than he would ever admit. "But that doesn't mean she has to be so annoying."

"She's your little sister. That's her job."

Cordelia lifted the drop cloth, hoping to see a

trapdoor like the one that led to Elijah's office. All she found was a nest of house centipedes. Three of them skittered past her foot, causing her to do an embarrassing little dance to avoid them. She turned toward Benji, hoping he hadn't noticed, and saw him pushing on different spots in a wall.

"I think I have something here," he said.

There was a tiny *click*, and the wall swung open on a hidden hinge.

"Ta-da!" he exclaimed. "I noticed this basement is a lot smaller than the other ones, so I figured there must be more behind this wall. It's a magnetic latch, like the kind they have on cabinets. You just need to push it in the right spot." He almost looked disappointed. "It would have been nice if there was a secret lever or something. These guys might be top-of-the-line when it comes to technology, but Elijah Shadow was way better at secret passageways."

Cordelia replaced the drop cloth where she'd found it and joined Benji at the entrance to the secret room. It was too dark to make much out.

Benji turned on the light.

16

The Hidden Cell

The liquid nitrogen freezer was right in front of them. Cordelia opened it and counted eight boo-tubes. They all looked empty to her, since she wasn't wearing her spectercles, but Benji was able to see Gideon's mist, as well as Mr. DeWitt's and Esmae's. This was definitely the place where Laurel stored the phantoms.

The three red doors were harder to explain.

They stood in the center of every wall except the one with the secret entrance. Next to each door was a metal panel, also red, that reminded Cordelia of the fuse box in her garage. During a heat wave the previous summer—when Ludlow had suffered a woeful number

184

of power outages–her dad had taught her how to oper-
ate it.

Benji rapped on a door with his knuckles.

"It's metal," he said. "Do we open it?"

"We're here. Might as well get our money's worth."

Benji listened at the door for a moment. "What if
there's something inside that we don't want to let out?"
he whispered.

"Like what?"

"I don't know. And I'd rather not start imagining
possibilities right now."

"Let's see what's behind here first," Cordelia said,
opening the small metal door. Inside were two rows of
switches, a USB port, and a cylindrical compartment
with a nozzle at the bottom.

"It looks like a boo-tube goes here," Cordelia said.

Before Benji had a chance to reply, they heard the
front door open. Floorboards squeaked.

"Seriously, Kyle," Laurel said. Cordelia peeked out
the secret door, ready to close it at a moment's notice.
"Mehar was so proud of this particular batch of videos.
She predicted a fifteen-minute turnaround, maybe even
less. Now she thinks I don't respect her work because
you left her thumb drive behind. You know how touchy
she can be, like all artists."

Cordelia had never had an actual conversation with Mehar, but she had seen her around the main office. Her job was curating the videos that were played on the life windows. This usually involved combing through any social-media accounts the ghost had left behind in order to locate family videos, favorite activities, and any other major interests.

"I'll text Mehar and apologize again," Laurel continued. "You get things rolling—and make it fast. I want to check on those kids. I don't like the way Cordelia was looking at me today."

Kyle's boots appeared at the top of the stairs. Cordelia pulled the secret door shut as quietly as possibly, wincing as the magnets clicked together. She backed into the room.

"Cordelia," Benji whispered, frantically waving her over. He had opened the red door next to the panel they had been investigating, and was now standing in a dark cell with enough space for both of them. Cordelia wanted to join him, but in order to do so she would have to cross the entire room.

She could hear Kyle's footsteps growing closer. There was no time.

She opened the door behind her and stepped inside. It was an empty cell that looked identical to Benji's. There was no light, no window. When she shut the door, it became too dark to see the fingers in front of her face.

Click. The secret door swung open.

Kyle was here.

Cordelia clasped a hand over her mouth to muffle the sound of her breathing. If Kyle opened the door, there was nowhere to hide. Her only hope was to stay quiet and pray he didn't look. She fought the instinctive urge to back away. It wasn't like there were any hiding spots in the cell, and moving would only increase the chance she made some sort of noise. She waited. And listened. Kyle opened the metal panel and then, judging from the swish of cloth and jingle of keys, got something out of his pocket. Cordelia's money was on the thumb drive. She heard another sound that might have been him entering it into the USB slot, and then the click of a switch.

He had turned something on, she was sure of it. But as far as Cordelia could tell, nothing in the room had changed.

"You done yet?" Laurel called from upstairs.

"It's downloading!" Kyle screamed. And then, under his breath, "How many times have we done this?"

It seemed fair to assume that Kyle was downloading Mehar's videos. But to where? There weren't any life windows in this house. And what had they done with Dr. Gill's boo-tube?

I'll figure all that out later, Cordelia thought, doing her best to inhale and exhale as quietly as possible. The important thing was that Kyle had shown no inclination to open any of the red doors. As long as Benji and Cordelia stayed quiet, they should be safe.

Kyle had just begun to sing some country song when Cordelia felt a cold prick at the back of her hand, like being touched by an icicle. She knew what it was immediately. On her very first day at Shadow School she had been touched by a ghost, and it wasn't the kind of thing you forgot.

She wasn't alone in the cell.

Kyle was really getting into his song now—judging from the rhythmic clicking of his heels, Cordelia suspected there might be some dancing involved as well. She was grateful; it helped mask the sound as she removed her spectercles from her pocket and put them on.

Dr. Gill was sitting on the floor in front of her, as though they were about to play a game of patty cake or share secrets during a sleepover. The light that surrounded her had a pinkish hue. In the past, Dr. Gill had been the calmest of ghosts, but now there was a wild pleading in her eyes, as though she had lost something important and expected Cordelia to find it.

"I'm sorry," Cordelia mouthed. "I don't know what you want."

Dr. Gill didn't like that. She leaned forward, pressing her hands against the floor for balance, until their faces were only inches apart. Cordelia closed her eyes, then changed her mind and opened them again. No matter what, it was better to see. The ghost raised a finger and pointed at Cordelia, then used the same finger to point at the walls. When Cordelia didn't react, Dr. Gill repeated the motion a second time, with rising anger in her eyes. It was clear she wanted Cordelia to do something—but what?

"I don't know," Cordelia mouthed. "I don't know."

Dr. Gill went through the same routine a third time, though she wasn't pointing now—she was jabbing. Cordelia bit her lower lip. She couldn't make a sound. Kyle was right outside her door, singing his stupid song. He would hear her. And while her mind was still struggling to make sense of what, exactly, was happening, Cordelia had an instinctive feeling that Laurel and Kyle would be very angry if they found her here.

Dr. Gill moved closer. A wisp of gray hair passed through Cordelia's chin. It was like being struck by sleet.

Kyle stopped singing.

"It's done!" he shouted.

Cordelia was suddenly surrounded by dozens of videos, each wall—and the ceiling—revealing itself to be a life window. She recognized most of them from Dr. Gill's house: a tropical island being filmed from the deck of a boat; someone making a *vroom, vroom* sound as he rolled a toy train past a clapping baby; Dr. Gill feeding her new husband from their tooth-shaped wedding cake. The images were disorienting, the sound deafening. The ghost's eyes filled with bliss as she went from one wall to the next, drinking in these digitalized fragments of her life.

What is this? Cordelia wondered. She was glad that Dr. Gill had completely forgotten about her, but that didn't make the barrage of images any less disturbing.

Someone banged on the door.

"Cordelia," Benji said. He had to shout to be heard over the videos. "They left. You can come out now."

Cordelia turned the doorknob. It didn't budge. Benji tried it from his end as well with no luck.

"It's locked!" he exclaimed. "That's weird. Mine stayed open. Let me flick some of these switches and see what they do!"

The life windows started to go dark, one by one. Dr. Gill gave a silent scream of rage and took a threatening step in Cordelia's direction.

"Switch them back!" Cordelia screamed. "Switch them back!"

The videos returned. Dr. Gill's attention was immediately redirected.

"Kyle must have the key," Cordelia said. "You have to get it somehow."

"But why would he lock your door and not–"

"I don't know! Just get me out of here!"

"Okay, hang tight. I'll grab Agnes and see what we can do."

"Hurry!"

Cordelia waited. Watching the videos began to make her stomach churn, so she pressed her back against a wall and focused on the floor. Waited. But still she could hear them, a dozen moments existing simultaneously: bat cracks, band plays, crowd roars, dog barks, group laughs. Cordelia clapped her hands over her ears. Waited. *Hurry up hurry up HURRY UP.* At least Dr. Gill seemed content for now. Cordelia could only see the ghost from behind, but her body was perfectly still as she watched a little girl ride a carousel.

Is her neck longer?

At first Cordelia thought it was just a trick of the constantly shifting light, but no–Dr. Gill's neck was definitely a good six inches longer than before. That wasn't the only difference. Instead of her bathrobe, she was now wearing a white lab coat.

Cordelia pulled out her phone and texted Benji.

Something weird happening get me out NOW.

The video of the little girl changed to some kind of dental procedure. Cordelia saw a flash of gums and blood and looked away. A few moments later, she took a quick glance and saw that Dr. Gill's neck had grown again. It was almost a foot long now. She barely looked human anymore.

Phantom, Cordelia thought. *She's changing into a phantom.*

She slid along the wall, staying as far away as possible, until she could see part of the dentist's face. Her head tottered from side to side on its newly elongated neck like a balloon in the wind. There was a perfect set of tiny teeth around the inside of her left eye socket.

Cordelia returned to her previous spot on the other side of the cell and texted Benji again. This time there were many more exclamation marks.

She waited.

Dr. Gill didn't move, but the pink light that surrounded her was beginning to grow dim. Cordelia suspected that when it vanished completely, the ghost's transformation into a phantom would be complete.

Come on, Benji. Where are you?

She twisted the doorknob with two hands, in case

she had developed superpowers since her last try, but her palms were so sweaty that she couldn't get a good grasp. For a long time, no one moved—until Dr. Gill tilted her head, like someone hearing a distant sound. Slowly, she began to turn around.

Cordelia's vision blurred. She couldn't see a thing.

"No," she said, smacking the spectercles like a broken vending machine. "Not now. No!"

The blurriness was making her dizzy. Cordelia had no choice.

She removed the spectercles.

Dr. Gill was invisible. Maybe she was still standing in the same spot. Maybe not. There was no way to tell. Cordelia listened carefully, hoping her ears might give her a clue, and heard a strange new sound rise over the din of the life windows. It took her a moment to identify it, but when she did, Cordelia's terror grew to new heights.

It was a whir of a dental drill.

There was a *plink*, like a pebble striking glass. The life window directly across from her shattered.

Cordelia pounded on the door with two fists. "Help!" she screamed at the top of her lungs. "Anyone! Help! Help!"

Two more *plinks*. Two more life windows. Closer this time. With fewer videos, the room grew darker. Quieter too—though the drill eagerly filled this vacated pocket of sound. Cordelia could hear it clearly now, conjuring unwelcome images of sitting in the dentist's chair. She felt something cold pass across her lips, ghostly fingers searching for purchase, eager to expose teeth and get to work.

Plink.

The life window next to her went dark.

"Help! Help!"

The door swung open. Cordelia fell forward into the glorious light. Someone caught her. The sound of the dental drill—close, far too close—was suddenly cut off as the door slammed shut.

"Just in time," she said, turning around and expecting to see Benji's face.

It was Laurel.

Betrayal

Without a word, Laurel led Cordelia upstairs. Kyle was leaning against the front door with his arms crossed. Cordelia had escaped the cell, but she was still trapped.

Benji and Agnes were sitting on the floor with their heads down, like loved ones in a hospital waiting room expecting the worst. The moment Cordelia came up the stairs, their looks of concern transformed to relief. Agnes hugged her tight.

"You're okay!" she exclaimed. "We were so worried!"

"Sorry, Cord," Benji said. "It was taking us forever to get the keys, and your messages were freaking us out, so we didn't think we could risk waiting. We told them what happened."

"You did the right thing," Cordelia said. "Another few seconds in there and . . . I honestly don't know what would have happened. But I don't think I'm ever going to the dentist again."

There was a loud crashing noise as Laurel tossed a mannequin from the dining room into the living room.

Cordelia let out a scream that would have won her the role in any horror movie. "Sorry," she said, embarrassed. "Rough day."

Laurel chucked another mannequin. Its arm split off and spun across the floor. Cordelia hoped this was a sign that she would be taking out her anger on inanimate objects and not them.

"Freaking Kenny," Laurel said, making short work of the last mannequin. "The whole idea behind these things was to scare anyone away who wasn't supposed to be here. Because . . . mannequins. But Kenny likes to come here on his lunch break and dress them up and move them around. He thinks he's a riot. Every office has their Kenny, you know?"

Cordelia didn't know, but she nodded anyway. Laurel was scaring her right now, and she was ready to agree with anything she said.

"Sit," Laurel said, pointing at the upside-down milk

crates set around the table. "All of you."

They took the mannequins' former spots. Cordelia peeked at the cards left facedown on the table and saw that her mannequin had been sitting on a royal flush. Kenny was apparently a stickler for detail.

"This is an unneeded complication," Laurel said with an annoyed huff. "Why couldn't you have just done your jobs and minded your own business? Now everything is *ruined*."

"What did you see?" Benji asked Cordelia.

"She's turning ghosts into phantoms."

Agnes, ever the scientist, asked, "How?"

"It was an accident," Laurel said. "Shady Rest was my grandfather's baby, as you know, and I wanted to bring something new to the business, my own twist. So I came up with the life windows." Laurel's eyes lit up. "The first day we turned them on, and Victor told us how much the ghosts loved them, Grandpa said he had never been so proud of me. I thought that was the end of it. Just a little something extra to keep our residents happy. But then they started to change. And I knew I'd happened upon something even more special than I'd suspected."

Benji shook his head, trying to make sense of what he had just heard. "Watching the videos changes ghosts into phantoms?"

Laurel broke into a proud grin and nodded. Now that the kids knew the truth, she seemed eager to share the details of her discovery.

"You know how a ghost normally turns into a phantom, right?" Laurel asked.

"Jealousy," said Cordelia, who was done trying to conceal her knowledge. "The more time they spend haunting this world, the more they dream of being a part of it again. Eventually, it transforms them, like a disease."

"Very good," Laurel said. "There's one problem with the old-fashioned way of doing things, though. It takes *forever*. Fifty, sixty, seventy years. Maybe even centuries."

Elijah was right after all, Cordelia thought.

"My way works the same, more or less. All I did was accelerate the process. Our residents are hit twenty-four/seven with all the things they loved in life and can never do again. Favorite places. Favorite foods. Favorite people. Through the social-media channels, they're forced to watch their families and loved ones move on without them. How could they not be consumed by jealousy? I don't give them a choice in the matter."

Cordelia felt sick to her stomach. The ghosts weren't being comforted by the life windows. They were being tormented by them. And she had done nothing to stop it.

"You're a monster," she said.

"I'm just giving nature a little kick in the butt to move things along," Laurel said. "It's the same as sprinkling fertilizer on your grass to make it grow better."

"Why do you put them in those horrible cells?" Cordelia asked. She turned to Benji and Agnes to explain. "Dr. Gill was in there with me. Her videos were playing everywhere. But if the life windows in her house were already turning her into a phantom, why bother with all that?"

"We could leave the ghosts in their homes," Laurel said. "But that would require us to capture them after they've turned into phantoms. As you know, that can be difficult. The phantom cell itself is a type of ghost tent, so all we have to do is turn a switch and they get sucked back into their boo-tube. Easy. Besides, that final step is always the most difficult one. It often takes months for them to turn into a phantom after they start glowing—and sometimes it never happens at all. Hitting them with all those videos at once is the little push they need to get over that final hump."

"If that's the case, why not just put them in the cell from the start?" Agnes asked.

"They need to be acclimated first, otherwise all

those memories and experiences overload their fragile little systems. When they start glowing, we know they're ready. If we put them in the phantom cell too early . . . poof! Bye, bye, ghostie. Then, when they're good and ripe, Kyle leaves the boo-tubes in our preselected houses. Are you wondering how?" She mimed holding a phone to her ear. "It's usually Trish who takes care of this part. She might not be the sharpest tool in the shed, but she's quite the phone actress. It goes something like this: 'Good afternoon, this is Lisa from PDO Contractors. Your house has been randomly selected for five hundred dollars' worth of free home repair! Just pick a project you'd like us to take care of, and I'll send my best handyman over there as soon as next week.'"

"PDO," Agnes said. She laughed bitterly. "Phantom Drop-Off."

"It's the second call that seals the deal, though," Laurel continued. "'Hi, this is Lisa again. I'm just calling to make sure you were happy with our repairs' they always are; we aim to please—'Oh dear! Is everything okay? What? You have a ghost in your house? Goodness gracious! Well, I actually *do* know someone who can help you—but I have to warn you, they're not cheap. What? Money is no object? Let me see if I can find that number. . . .'"

"It's almost four," Kyle said, checking his phone.

200

"These kids are going to be picked up soon. We need a decision."

Cordelia didn't like the sound of that. "Decision about what?" she asked.

Laurel put her hands on her hips. "I don't appreciate the way you three are looking at me right now, like I'm the bad guy or something. That's not fair. Do you think I want things to be like this? I would have been so much happier continuing Grandpa's business the way he always ran it. But he didn't leave me any money! At the end, he was writing checks to twenty charities a day, just trying to get rid of it all. He donated fifteen thousand dollars to help save the saola!"

"What's a saola?" Benji asked.

"Exactly! I adored my grandfather, and I want nothing more than to preserve his vision by helping as many ghosts as possible. But nothing comes without a cost."

"You're not helping ghosts," Cordelia said. "You're turning them into monsters."

"For now," Laurel said. "Once I have enough to keep the money-making division of Shady Rest running smoothly, I'll focus on rescue operations again. But we have to keep the coffers full. I have a staff to pay and new houses to build." She took the deck of cards off the table and idly began to shuffle them. "So, now you know where I stand. The next decision is entirely yours.

Do you want to be a part of this or not?"

"Is that what you asked Victor when he found out what you were really doing here?" Cordelia asked—and immediately wished she could take the words back. Was bringing up Victor—who had mysteriously vanished—really the best idea right now?

Laurel threw her head back and laughed.

"Do you honestly think Victor was shocked and offended by the idea of hurting the ghosts? Please. I couldn't have created this system without his help. He was in it from the start. Don't paint him as an innocent here."

"Then why did he leave?"

"Because in the end, he didn't care about Grandpa's vision. All Victor wanted was money. And that's not why I'm here. I truly want to help the ghosts. The phantoms are just an end to a beautiful means."

"I don't believe you," Cordelia said. "I've seen all your expensive jewelry. The nice car you drive."

"Believe what you want. You in or out?"

"What happens if we say no?" Benji asked.

"Then I replace you. It's not like you two are the only people in the world who can see ghosts. I had a feeling things might end up this way, so I already have a few feelers out there."

"Three minutes," Kyle said.

"You seriously expect us to believe that you're just going to let us go?" Cordelia asked.

"Why not? You know as well as I do that telling anyone is pointless—they'll never believe you, and there's no way to prove it." Laurel rolled her eyes. "Did you think I was going to murder you or something? Seriously, Cordelia. Could you be any more dramatic? I'm practical, not evil."

"Laurel . . ." Kyle said.

"I know, I know! Their parents. So what's it going to be, kids?"

Agnes leaned forward. "First of all, a saola is a mammal that lives in Vietnam and is sometimes referred to as the Asian unicorn. Second, we all quit."

The kids got to their feet. Kyle, remarkably, opened the front door and stepped to the side. It seemed as though the decision really was theirs to make. Cordelia knew they would be back to help the ghosts, but after they talked to Dr. Roqueni. Right now, she just wanted to get out of there.

Cordelia had just stepped outside when she noticed that Benji was no longer with them. She turned around and saw him standing in the middle of the living room with a pensive expression.

"Benji?" she asked.

"I think I'm going to keep working here."

Cordelia waited for the punch line, but his face was as serious as she'd ever seen it.

"You've heard what she's doing," Cordelia said. "They're changing ghosts into phantoms! You can't be okay with that!"

"I'm not. But I can learn to live with it."

"Benji!"

"My family really needs the money, Cordelia. They're counting on me!"

"You said things were better."

"I lied, okay? I didn't want you to feel bad. Things are worse than ever. The only thing that's keeping us afloat is the money I make here. I can't stop. I just can't."

Laurel, who had been watching their exchange with clear amusement, said, "Why don't you run along, Cordelia? Tell your mom or dad that I'll give Benji a lift home later. We have to talk about some changes we'll be making now that he's working solo." She wrapped an arm around his shoulder. "How does a raise sound, for starters?"

Benji brightened. "That sounds good."

Agnes gave Benji a final glare of her own and led Cordelia down the front walk. "Come on," Agnes said. "He's made his choice. There's nothing we can do about it." Cordelia bit her lower lip, fighting to keep the tears from streaming down her face. She couldn't believe this was actually happening.

They started across the street. Laurel, Kyle, and Benji emerged from the house. Laurel was talking to Benji in a soft voice.

Cordelia stopped in the middle of the street and faced them.

"Benji Núñez!" she exclaimed. "If you stay here, we are no longer friends!"

"I'm sorry you feel that way," Benji said, and got into the back seat of Laurel's car. Kyle gunned the engine and the car blew past Cordelia and Agnes. Benji didn't even look in their direction as he passed.

18

Dr. Roqueni's Return

Cordelia lay on the basement sofa, staring into space. It was beginning to get dark out, but the light switch was all the way on the other side of the room, an insurmountable distance. Maybe when it was dark, she could fall asleep. At least that way she could forget about Benji for a little while.

She was just starting to close her eyes when her parents came downstairs and asked her what was wrong. Cordelia told them Benji was a jerk. Her parents exchanged a knowing look and told Cordelia they could get takeout from her favorite restaurant for dinner. Then they each kissed her on the cheek.

Mr. Liu turned on the lights as they left.

Cordelia was left alone with her thoughts. She knew she should be trying to figure out a way to help the ghosts of Shady Rest before Laurel turned them all into phantoms, but at this particular moment, she was having trouble caring. All she could think about was Benji. Maybe it had been too harsh of her to say they could no longer be friends. Cordelia's family wasn't rich by any stretch of the imagination, but both her parents were employed, and she had never lacked for anything she needed. What right did she have to judge Benji for doing something morally questionable in order to help his own family? If their situations were reversed, maybe she would do the same thing.

No, Cordelia thought. *I wouldn't.*

That would make her no better than Laurel, who believed her cruel actions were excusable because she helped ghosts as well as hurt them. That wasn't the way it worked. You did good things, or you did bad things. She understood that Benji loved his family, but that didn't make what he was doing right.

I can never forgive him for this, she thought.

Sometime later, after it had gone full dark, Mrs. Liu came back downstairs. She was wearing her regular Saturday attire of black yoga pants and T-shirt. Her blond hair was tied in a ponytail.

"Benji's at the door," she said.

Cordelia shot up from the couch. *"What?"*

"I can tell him to get lost," Mrs. Liu said in a tone that suggested doing so would give her a great deal of pleasure. "Did he start dating that other girl again? Is that what this is about?"

"No! For the last time, we're just friends."

Mrs. Liu didn't look convinced. "I've seen the way you look at him. You will never be 'just friends' with that boy."

"Mom. Can you just send him down? Please?"

"Let me check to make sure your dad hasn't killed him first. If I don't come right back, we're hiding the body."

While Mrs. Liu went to retrieve Benji, Cordelia hurriedly straightened the pillows on the couch so he couldn't tell she'd been lying there like a pathetic mess. She started to finger-comb her hair, which was sticking up all over the place, then got annoyed at herself for bothering and messed it up again.

Benji came downstairs. There was a big smile on his face.

"Hey!" he said. "I texted you like a thousand times. Why didn't you respond?"

Cordelia had expected Benji to be apologetic, and his cheery attitude annoyed her. "I turned off my phone.

After everything that happened, I didn't feel like—"

Before Cordelia could finish her sentence, Benji hugged her tight.

"You were *amazing*," he said. "Laurel fell for it hook, line, and sinker. She totally thinks you're mad at me, which just made her believe my story even more."

Cordelia stared at him, trying to make sense of what was happening.

"Umm," she managed. "What do you—"

"It was so cool that we didn't need to even talk about it," Benji said. He tapped his temple. "Great minds think alike! You knew exactly what I was trying to do and just went with it. If we're going to stop Shady Rest, we need someone on the inside. Agnes isn't an option because she can't see the ghosts. And it can't be you, because Laurel would never buy that. It has to be me. I didn't like using my family as the reason for staying, but it worked like a charm."

None of it was real, Cordelia thought. *It was all an act!*

"So your family is actually doing better, right?" she asked. "Like you said in the basement?"

"Yeah, yeah. We're fine. So I know we should wait until we all get together before coming up with a plan, but I have a really good idea. . . ." He hesitated and narrowed his eyes. "You look completely stunned right

209

now. It's like you thought"—his face fell—"you didn't think I wanted to keep working in that terrible place for real, did you?"

Cordelia didn't know how to respond, so she kissed him instead. Benji was so stunned that he forgot all about his question. Judging from the dumbfounded look on his face, Cordelia wondered if he even remembered his name.

"You kissed me," he said.

"Uh-huh," Cordelia replied, a little shocked herself. "That's okay, right?"

"Very okay."

"Good. Great."

Cordelia took a seat on the couch. Benji sat next to her. They were both a little dazed.

"This has been a very eventful day," Cordelia said.

"It hasn't been boring. Do you want to hear my idea now?"

Cordelia thought about it and shook her head. "I don't want to talk about the ghosts. I just want to sit here for a little while."

Benji took her hand.

"Finally," he said.

Dr. Roqueni returned two weeks later.

They decorated Darius's office with a Welcome

Home banner and a few balloons. Agnes was too busy with another project to make brownies, so Cordelia and Benji baked chocolate-chip cookies together. They got a little distracted at one point and ended up burning a batch, but the rest of the cookies turned out surprisingly well.

Dr. Roqueni arrived just after school ended, wearing a chic blue dress with a foreign cut. She looked five years younger.

"I've missed you all so much," she said, hugging them one at a time.

She had a tote bag full of souvenirs wrapped in brightly colored tissue paper. Agnes got a box of fancy chocolates from Switzerland, Benji a Real Madrid jersey, and Cordelia a keychain from the Château de Puymartin. Dr. Roqueni told her that it was a famous French castle haunted by a ghost known as the White Lady. Cordelia pretended that she hadn't already known that.

"There's a second part to your present," the principal whispered to her when no one else was listening. "But that will have to wait for now."

Once everyone had settled in, they spent a good hour looking at photos and listening to Dr. Roqueni's stories. A lot of them involved Mr. Shadow. The guarded tones with which Dr. Roqueni usually spoke of her uncle had been replaced by genuine affection, making Cordelia believe that the rift between them had finally been mended. This should have been a cause for celebration, but it broke Cordelia's heart. If Mr. Shadow had indeed betrayed them, the blow would now be twice as devastating to his poor niece. She might never trust anyone again.

Mr. Shadow had passed on the party so he could catch up on his sleep, which was a great relief. Cordelia wasn't sure she could face him right now and pretend everything was okay. It also meant they could update the principal and Mr. Derleth without the risk of being spied upon.

"This is embarrassing," Dr. Roqueni said after telling them a story about getting lost in Edinburgh. "I've been going on and on about myself. What's new in your lives?"

Cordelia wasn't going to get a better segue than that. She knew she couldn't put it off any longer.

"Do you remember those two ghost catchers we met at Gideon's Ark?" Cordelia asked. "The ones you specifically told us not to contact?"

"Yes," Dr. Roqueni said.

"Well, we contacted them. Surprise! It turns out they run a business called Shady Rest. . . ."

They told them everything. Dr. Roqueni and Mr. Derleth listened silently for the most part, asking for clarification on only a few points. The kids took turns talking, but even when Benji or Agnes was taking the lead, Dr. Roqueni's eyes kept returning to Cordelia. *She blames me*, Cordelia thought. *And why not? This was all my idea from the start.*

"How long has this been going on?" Mr. Derleth asked.

"Since January," Benji said.

Mr. Derleth's mouth froze in a big O, like a kid who had to open wide to take his medicine. "I had no idea."

"How could you have known?" Dr. Roqueni asked. "They only went on Saturdays."

"Cordelia hasn't mentioned the ghosts once since you left! That should have been a huge clue something was wrong. I just figured she'd discovered boys or something."

"Oh, she has!" Agnes exclaimed with delight. Cordelia smacked her on the arm while Benji blushed.

"I'm sure you're super mad at us right now," Cordelia said. "And we deserve it—me more than anyone. But for what it's worth, we're really sorry we didn't listen to you."

"I'm not mad," the principal said. "I'm disappointed. I thought, by now, the three of you would realize that when I tell you not to do something, it's because I have your best interests at heart. I care about you very much."

Agnes lowered her head. "It would be better if you yelled at us."

"I can yell at you," Mr. Derleth suggested.

"We're good," said Benji.

"What's done is done," Dr. Roqueni said. "Right now we need to worry about what comes next. I know you want to help these ghosts—as do I—but this Laurel sounds dangerous. She's given you the option of walking away. Perhaps you should take it."

"No way," Cordelia said. "What they're doing to the poor ghosts is terrible enough, but I'm also worried about the living. Eventually, one of these phantoms is going to kill someone. We need to stop them before that happens."

Cordelia expected Dr. Roqueni to argue with her, but instead the principal gave a reluctant nod. "I see your point. It's unfortunate, but having the Sight does bestow a certain responsibility on you and Benji. That doesn't mean we should be foolhardy, however. Benji— are you sure it's a good idea to keep going back there on your own?"

"That's the only way our plan will work. I've been taking what we need from the supply shed, a little at a time, and on the actual day of the—"

A grinding noise reverberated throughout the office; someone was opening the trapdoor. Cordelia shared a panicked look with her friends.

No! she thought. *We were supposed to have more time to explain!*

"Oh, good," Dr. Roqueni said with a look of delight. "Uncle Darius is here! He'll be so excited to see you. And I'm sure he'll have some good ideas about what to do next."

Cordelia had to act fast. In a moment or two, Mr. Shadow would walk into the office. They couldn't risk trusting him. If he was working with Laurel, their entire plan would be ruined.

"Don't tell Mr. Shadow about any of this," she said, her eyes imploring Dr. Roqueni to trust her. "We think he might be part of it."

"Impossible. My uncle would never—"

"You told us not to trust him," Agnes said. "You were right."

Darius Shadow entered the office. Like his niece, he looked rejuvenated by their time together.

"Sorry I'm late," he said, stifling a yawn. "When you get to be my age, jet lag is murder. What did I miss?"

"Dr. Roqueni was telling us some cool stories," Benji said. "Sounds like you had a great time."

"Greatest trip of my life."

He smiled at Dr. Roqueni. She managed a smile in return, but Cordelia could read the uncertainty in her eyes. It had taken her a long time to trust her uncle again, and now they were asking her to throw it all away.

"You have any stories for us, Mr. Shadow?" Agnes asked.

"Oh, I'm sure I can come up with one or two," Mr. Shadow said, taking a seat on the couch and crossing his legs. He bounced his fedora on one knee. "Let me see. There was this one time we got lost in Edinburgh–"

"I've already told them that one," Dr. Roqueni said. "Besides, the children have a far more interesting story to tell. It seems the three of them joined the workforce while we were away. Helping ghosts, if you can believe it!"

The kids stared at the principal in disbelief.

Agnes said, "Umm . . . I'm sure Mr. Shadow is way too tired to hear about that right now."

"I disagree," Dr. Roqueni said. The uncertainty in her eyes had vanished. "This simply can't wait, and I want to hear his opinion. I *trust* him. Totally and completely."

Cordelia crossed over to the snack table and nervously ate three cookies while Dr. Roqueni gave a quick summary of what they had just told her. Mr. Shadow looked completely shocked, as though this was the first time he had ever heard of a place called Shady Rest.

Maybe we were wrong, Cordelia thought, willing it to be true. *There could be a perfectly reasonable explanation for why he was at Mr. Knox's funeral . . .*

No.

Just because she wanted Mr. Shadow to be innocent didn't make it true. The facts were the facts. Laurel had planted a phantom in Gideon's Ark in order to draw Benji and Cordelia out. How else could she have known about them? It had to have been Mr. Shadow. He was the only connection between Shadow School and Shady Rest.

Cordelia's brain found the logic difficult to deny— and yet her heart still resisted it.

She had to know for sure. After thinking about it for a moment (and eating one last cookie), Cordelia decided to try a test. She waited for an opportune moment in the conversation and said, "It sounds like things were a lot different when the original owner of Shady Rest was around, but he died last year." She focused on Mr. Shadow so she could gauge his reaction to her next words. "His name was Leland Knox."

Mr. Shadow's mouth fell open.

"*Leland's* mixed up in all this?"

Cordelia felt like cheering. If Mr. Shadow had wanted to keep his connection to Shady Rest a secret, he would have denied knowing Mr. Knox. Instead, he told the truth, which hopefully meant he had nothing to hide. Cordelia wasn't quite ready to exonerate him completely, but it was a promising sign.

Benji and Agnes, clearly thinking along the same lines, looked eager to learn more.

"How do you know Mr. Knox?" Benji asked.

"We met years ago, before Aria was even born. Leland shared my ghost obsession. At one point we were inseparable, but we had a bit of a falling out. It was my fault. I was a different man back then, and I dragged Leland into some shady business. After that he wanted nothing to do with me. Years later, he became a very successful businessman and philanthropist—which didn't surprise me one bit. Leland was the kind of guy who would have given a total stranger the shirt off his back."

"He never told you about Shady Rest?" Cordelia asked.

"No. I can't say I blame him. After what I did, I wouldn't have trusted me either. Like I said, I was a different man. Besides, we hadn't spoken in close to forty years—until last July, that is. Leland called me out of the blue and asked me to come to the hospital. He didn't have much time left, but he wanted to tell me he forgave me so my heart would be at ease. Typical Leland, thinking of other people to the end. I know I shouldn't have, but I told him about Shadow School. I thought hearing about Brights and what awaits a good man like him on the other side might ease his passing a little."

"Did you mention me and Benji?" Cordelia asked.

"Not by name," Mr. Shadow said. "I did say there were two students with the Sight, but I hoped there were more in the lower grades since you were graduating this year." He tapped his chin with his index finger. "You know, Leland was just about to tell me something when his granddaughter ushered me out the door. I wonder if he was going to spill the beans about Shady Rest."

"Could be," Agnes said. "His granddaughter wouldn't have wanted you to know that. She's the one we've been talking about, by the way. Laurel."

"The one causing all the trouble?" asked Mr. Shadow. He didn't seem very surprised. "I didn't care for her. I thought she might have been eavesdropping on our conversation."

"Of course she was!" Cordelia exclaimed.

Suddenly, everything made sense. After listening to Mr. Shadow, Laurel knew there were two eighth graders at Shadow School who could see the ghosts. The timing was perfect. She desperately needed a replacement for Victor—and here were two of them, just waiting to be recruited! There was one problem, though. Mr. Shadow had never used their names, so she still needed to figure out their identities.

That's why she planted Gideon in the ark, Cordelia thought.

The phantom would cause the two mystery students to reveal themselves. They would act differently than the others. Stick out. Laurel made sure she was at the ark so she could watch out for them. She hadn't been hired to catch the phantom, and she certainly didn't care about helping the kids. Her only objective was to identify her two new employees.

Cordelia felt horrible for doubting Mr. Shadow. In the end, all he had done was tell an old friend a story.

"If nobody objects," Dr. Roqueni said. "I think it's time we hear Benji's mysterious idea. How are you planning to rescue all these ghosts without anyone stopping you?"

"Easy," Benji said. "We're going to steal them."

19

Heist

It was Cordelia's first time riding in the trunk of a car, and she was not enjoying the experience. Mr. Shadow liked to spend his weekends fishing in the summer, and even though he had removed all his equipment, the smell remained.

They hit a bump, and her sensitive stomach lurched in protest.

"Whee!" Agnes said. "I've always wanted to do this! Haven't you always wanted to do this?"

"I hate you," Cordelia said.

It was freakishly warm for May, and her T-shirt was already matted to her back. The space was tight with Agnes there, and no matter how much Cordelia twisted and turned, she couldn't find a comfortable spot.

The car rolled to a stop.

"I swear, you're seventy percent legs," Cordelia said. "It's unnatural."

"Quiet, short stuff. Mr. Shadow's talking to the guard."

They heard muffled voices. Mr. Shadow sounded like his usual cheery self. The guard's voice was flat and bored. That was good. A bored guard was far more likely to wave the car through without a second thought.

Just as Cordelia was beginning to wonder if something was wrong, she heard the *beeeep* of the boom gate rising. It sounded as lovely as a church bell. Mr. Shadow bade the guard a good day and drove into the village.

"See?" Agnes said. "I knew it would work."

"That was the easy part."

The car squeaked to a halt, and Mr. Shadow opened the trunk. Cordelia leaped out and took a deep breath of open air. They were behind the main office in a little lot where the employees parked. There was a back door and three windows. Benji had lowered all the blinds, but Cordelia thought they should hurry, just in case.

While Mr. Shadow helped Agnes out, warning her not to hit her head on the trunk, Cordelia unloaded the bags from the back seat. There were four of them. The first three were bookbags packed to the brim with empty boo-tubes. They were heavier than they looked, but not nearly as heavy as the duffel bag lying across the floor of the back seat. Cordelia was careful not to hit it against the door as she pulled it out of the car. If the thing inside broke, their entire plan fell apart.

The back door to the main office swung open.

Cordelia instinctively started to hide and then sighed with relief as Benji stepped through the door. He had arrived at Shady Rest before them for his regularly scheduled workday.

"Did Laurel fall for it?" Cordelia asked, keeping her voice to a whisper. One of the windows above them was open a crack, and she didn't know how far their voices would carry.

"They left first thing this morning," Benji said. "It's a four-hour drive, even if they don't hit any traffic—which they hopefully will. They should be gone for the entire day."

Dr. Roqueni had called Shady Rest the day before, claiming that she owned a mansion on the coast of Maine that had "gotten itself haunted." She'd requested that Laurel come and investigate at once, and promised a hefty fee for simply showing up the next day. Since Laurel wanted to stretch this out into multiple paid visits, she had no need of Benji this time. She would just show up, tell the woman what she wanted to hear, and collect her fee.

"Laurel is going to be furious when she finds out it was a trick," Cordelia said.

"I'm really broken up about that," Benji said. He tossed Cordelia the ring of keys they normally used when doing ghost checks around the village. "I unlocked all the doors last weekend so we could get in and out faster, but just in case I missed one."

"Good idea," Cordelia said.

Benji looked over the bookbags. "Which one has the fakes for the freezer? I want to make sure we don't take it by accident."

"That one."

Benji tossed it over his shoulder and grabbed a second bookbag as well. "Come on, Ag. You're all set up. I just couldn't find the gloves."

"I'm sure they're around."

Benji closed the door behind him. As Cordelia threw the final bookbag over her shoulder, she heard an approaching car.

"Hide," Mr. Shadow whispered.

Cordelia grabbed the duffel bag and ran around the side of the house. A moment later, a red sports car blasting dance music swerved into a parking spot. Carl exited. Cordelia hadn't seen him since overhearing his conversation with Laurel about the Landmark Inn. His cheesy goatee had been replaced with an even cheesier mustache.

He regarded Mr. Shadow with suspicion.

"What are you doing back here?"

Mr. Shadow slipped into the persona of a doddering old man. "I have an appointment," he said, talking slower than usual and walking with a slight hunch in his back. "Name's Floyd Barrows. My dear old Gladys passed last summer, and she's chosen to stick around a little longer than I'm comfortable with. I've heard you can help with that sort of thing."

Carl's eyes narrowed with suspicion.

"How exactly did you hear of us?"

"I was on a golf retreat at a place called the Landmark Inn. Trying to get over my heartbreak with a little tee time, you know. The manager there slipped me your number. He said you did good work for them."

Mr. Shadow sold the story well, and Carl seemed to buy it. He might place a call to the Landmark later as confirmation, and that was just fine. Dr. Roqueni had already explained the entire story to Derek. After finding out how badly Laurel had taken advantage of him—and endangered his guests—he was eager to help.

"Just move your car to the front," Carl said, already walking away. It was clear he thought every minute spent talking to this old man was a minute wasted.

"This lot is for employees only. Trish will help you at the front desk."

"Sure thing," Mr. Shadow said, getting back into his car. He gave Cordelia a wink and drove out of the parking lot.

Benji returned shortly afterward. They made sure the coast was clear, then ran across the street to the brown ranch. The door was unlocked, as Benji had promised. Cordelia put the duffel bag down the moment they entered the house. The weight of it was already beginning to make her shoulder burn.

"Agnes is safe back there, right?" Cordelia asked, raising her voice to be heard over the sound of the life windows.

"Totally," Benji said. "The only people who ever go into the freezer room are Laurel and Kyle, and they should be in a different state by now. Once Agnes grabs the regular boo tubes, she'll head over to the second freezer and get the phantoms."

"It's a good plan," Cordelia said.

"Thanks. Let's get started."

Benji searched for the ghost while Cordelia put on her spectercles and waited for her eyes to adjust. It was the first time she had worn them since their ill-timed glitch with Dr. Gill, and she hoped they would last the entire day without a similar episode. After that, she suspected she might be done with them. Unless she could see the ghosts with her own eyes, she didn't want to see them at all.

"Up here!" Benji called.

The ghost was in her usual spot, watching a video of a chubby toddler trying to pin a Christmas bow on a cat. Cordelia had always thought the video was cute. Now that she knew its true purpose, however, even the boy's innocent giggles seemed menacing.

Benji and Cordelia stared down at the duffel bag.

"You ready to give this thing a whirl?" he asked.

They had known from the start that they wouldn't be able to use Laurel's ghost-catching equipment, which she always kept in a special safe, so Benji had stolen the dusty prototype in the storage shed. The hope was Agnes could fix it. It hadn't been easy. After a week of failed attempts, she had finally come up with the idea of combining the faulty machine with one of Elijah's architectural models. The result, which Cordelia now pulled out of the duffel bag, was a strange hybrid: a cute yellow cottage attached to a black box with several switches and a nozzle on one end.

"Agnes is sure we don't need a ghost tent with this one?" Benji asked.

"That's what she said."

"Did she ever get a chance to test it?" Benji asked.

"No time. She just finished it last night."

"Ugh."

"She said it will probably work, but there's also a 'slight possibility' it will explode. I think she was joking."

Benji had found entire boxes of boo-tubes collecting dust in the storage shed, so they had more than enough. He took a tube out of the bookbag now, fitted it onto the nozzle, and flicked a switch. The machine made an unhealthy clanking noise, like nails in a blender.

The kids shared an uneasy look.

"I'm sure it's fine," Cordelia said.

Benji pushed the doorbell.

The clanking returned, even louder than before, then settled into a rhythmic whir. Slowly but surely, the ghost turned into mist, swirled down the chimney of the yellow cottage, and finished up in the boo-tube.

"I never doubted Agnes for a second," Benji said.

"Me either."

Benji had hidden two bikes behind the house. Balancing the ghost catcher on the handlebars was a little tricky, but it was still easier than carrying it from house to house. This was a marathon, not a race, and they needed to conserve their energy. Besides, using bikes minimized the amount of time they'd be spending out in the open. It would be fine if someone saw Benji, but Cordelia no longer worked there. She had to stay out of sight.

"How long do you think it'll be before Laurel realizes the ghosts are gone?" Cordelia asked.

"It depends on how fast she replaces me after I quit. Laurel will never be able to tell on her own, since she can't see them. But once she finds someone with the Sight, our scam is up."

"At least it'll buy us some time to figure out a permanent solution."

Forty minutes later, Agnes caught up to them on a bike of her own. Her timing was perfect. They had accumulated five ghosts by that time, and though each boo-tube had been ensconced in its own protective sleeve, their collective heat could be felt through the lining of the bookbag.

"How did the ghost catcher work?" Agnes asked.

"Perfectly," Cordelia said, handing Agnes the bookbag. "Here's what we've nabbed so far."

"Yikes," Agnes said, feeling the heat. "I better get these to the freezer."

They couldn't leave the boo-tubes out in the open, or they would eventually melt and allow the ghosts to escape. That was Agnes's primary responsibility today. Every forty minutes, she would shuttle the captured ghosts back to the freezer, where their boo-tubes could cool down in preparation for the trip back to Shadow School.

"For round two," Agnes said, handing Benji a book-bag filled with empty boo-tubes.

Benji and Cordelia continued their rounds. There was one terrifying moment when Cordelia dropped the ghost catcher and the entire staircase of the cottage fell off, but it didn't seem to affect its performance.

When Agnes returned, they had seven boo-tubes for her.

"Did Mr. Shadow leave?" Benji asked.

"A while ago," Agnes said. "He has the first batch of ghosts you gave me and the boo-tubes I took from both freezers. I'm sure he's back at Shadow School by now."

Cordelia breathed a sigh of relief. Dr. Roqueni would place the boo-tubes in the mirror gallery, and when their inhabitants burned free, the dehaunter would send them into their Brights. Cordelia wished she could see it.

"How do the fakes look?" Benji asked.

"Perfect," said Agnes. "No one will ever know they've been switched."

Laurel might not be able to see the ghosts, but she could certainly see the boo-tubes; they couldn't simply take them without her noticing. Fortunately, you needed the Sight to see the spectral mist that swirled behind each window, so as long as they replaced each boo-tube with an identical match, she would never know the difference. Using photos Benji took while "working," they had duplicated each label exactly, and Mr. Shadow had even used his carpenter tools to replicate every ding and scratch.

The boo-tubes that now sat in the freezers were empty imposters.

Agnes checked her phone. "Mr. Derleth is probably here by now. What's his cover story again?"

"Poltergeist," Cordelia said. "Nice and simple. He doesn't lie as well as the Shadows."

"Halfway there," Benji said. "We can do this."

"See you in forty," Agnes said, biking away. "And you're right, Benji. I really think this is going to work!"

Cordelia felt the same way, but she wished Agnes hadn't said it out loud. Things were going so well, and she didn't want to jinx them.

Mr. Derleth came and left with two bookbags full of ghosts. Dr. Roqueni, who would be bringing Cordelia and Agnes to Shadow School along with the final boo-tubes, arrived at two on the dot. They were all starting to get tired—especially poor Agnes, who had probably biked ten miles by now—but the end was on the horizon.

There were only six ghosts left.

They entered the last of the white ranches. In the

kitchen, a teenage girl in a lacrosse uniform was watching one of her old high school games. A forest-green nimbus surrounded her.

"You're lucky," Benji told the ghost while they set up the machine. "A few weeks ago and you would have ended up in a phantom cell. Not fun. But instead you get to go to your Bright! What do you think, Cord? Lacrosse field?"

"We can do better than that. The most amazing lacrosse stadium that ever existed. With tons of people cheering for her in the stands."

"Where are we headed after this?" Benji asked.

"Back toward the main office, I think. You finish up. I'll figure out our next stop."

The light wasn't great inside the house, so Cordelia stepped outside to peruse the hand-drawn map they had made of Shady Rest. All the houses had been checked off except for a few nearby and one way up in the northeast corner of the village. Once they hit all those, they'd be done.

Not true, Cordelia thought. *What about the–*

She heard a voice in the distance and saw Trish cross the street at the end of the block. Cordelia froze in place. The receptionist was talking to someone on speakerphone and not looking in her direction. Any sudden movement might attract her attention.

". . . so yeah, Krista's going to be there, which isn't exactly ideal, but we can always leave early if . . ."

While switching the phone from one hand to the other, Trish spotted her. Cordelia's heart jumped in her chest. *Do I run? Do I try to talk my way out of this?* She waited for Trish to ask what she was doing there, or maybe sprint straight to the main office and make a full report, but instead the receptionist offered her a dismissive wave and kept walking. Cordelia couldn't believe her good fortune. Surely Laurel had informed her staff that Cordelia shouldn't be allowed in the village? Then again, maybe Trish had missed the email, or forgotten, or just didn't care. She seemed far more concerned with her phone conversation right now.

It'll be okay. It'll still be okay.

As Trish was about to disappear from view, however, she slowed down and took one final look in Cordelia's direction. It was hard to read her facial expression from this distance. Maybe it was just a casual glance. Or maybe Trish had finally remembered that Cordelia wasn't supposed to be there after all.

"Benji," Cordelia called through the open door. "I think we better hurry."

Benji and Cordelia were just about to enter a modern-looking house with cedar siding when Agnes came zipping down the street, pedaling like mad. She screeched to a halt in front of them. Sweat ran freely down her face, plastering her hair to her forehead. A fresh scratch ran down her arm.

"What happened?" Cordelia asked.

It took Agnes a few moments to catch her breath. "I had to take . . . evasive maneuvers. People . . . are looking for us."

Cordelia felt her stomach drop and immediately checked the street in both directions. It was all clear. For now.

"Guess Trish told everyone she saw you," Benji said. "That means Laurel probably knows by now too."

Agnes took the bookbag from Cordelia, wincing at the heat. Avoiding their pursuers had made her a few minutes late, and the boo-tubes were dangerously close to their breaking point. "I have to get these to the freezer, pronto. How many ghosts do you have left?"

"Two," Benji said. At the same time, Cordelia said, "Three."

"Which is it?" Agnes asked.

"*Two*," said Benji, imploring Cordelia not to make an issue of it.

"Maybe we should just let these last ones go," Agnes said. "Dr. Roqueni is in Carl's office right now, spinning a yarn about the ghost of her ex-husband. But her car is unlocked. We can hide in there until she's done."

"All we need is another ten minutes," Cordelia said.

"We're so close," Benji added. "We can't just abandon them."

Agnes gave them a teasing smile. "You two are adorable. We're getting ice cream after this, right?"

"You better believe it," Cordelia said.

Agnes rode off while Cordelia and Benji entered the next house. They captured the ghost in record time and were about to move on when they heard the rumble of a car engine. Peeking through the window, they saw a pickup truck pass at a turtle's crawl. There were two people kneeling on either side of the bed, scanning the street carefully: a lanky man Cordelia recognized as one of the grounds crew, and Mehar, the woman in charge of creating videos for the life windows.

"Agnes was right," Cordelia said. "They're on high alert."

"What do we do?" Benji asked.

"I can text Dr. Roqueni. Maybe she can swing by and pick us up. It might be hard to make it back to the main office right now without someone seeing us."

"And leave the last ghost behind? No way."

Despite her rising fear, Cordelia couldn't help but smile.

"I agree. I meant Dr. Roqueni could pick us up after

we get the last ghost, not before. Let's tell her to meet us there."

Before Cordelia could text the principal, however, they heard approaching voices. As quietly as they could, Benji and Cordelia slipped out the back door of the house just as the front one opened. They crossed to the next street and saw two cars parked at the curb—the pickup truck they had seen earlier and a blue car with a cracked headlight. The kids watched long enough to observe that several different groups were doing a house-by-house search, then timed a sprint into the narrow wooded area that ran through the center of the village.

"What about the bikes?" Cordelia asked.

"I'm sure they already found them by now," Benji said, wincing beneath the weight of the duffel bag. Despite Cordelia's suggestion that they share the burden, he had insisted on lugging it around the entire day. "Hopefully that'll throw them off and they'll search the houses back there twice as hard. We should stick to the woods. I'm pretty sure they bring us close to the last house."

"They do," Cordelia said, picturing the map of Shady Rest in her head. "Let's hope they don't think of looking in here."

"We'll just have to be quiet."

They headed north, trying to stay equally distant

from the houses on their left and Oak Lane, which ran parallel to the woods, on their right. When a car drove by, or they heard voices, the kids froze like cornered deer until the danger had passed. Even with the duffel bag, Benji was light on his feet and somehow managed to avoid making a single sound. Cordelia's feet, on the other hand, seemed magnetically attracted to every twig on their path.

It all worked out. Excluding scrapes and muddy sneakers, they reached the end of the woods unscathed.

They peeked between the branches. From here they had a perfect view of an ocean-blue house with a flat roof. Cordelia could see the ghost through the front window, an old man whose life windows were mostly views from aquarium webcams. He was currently entranced by a pair of sea lions.

To get to him, they only had to cross the street. Unfortunately, it was filled with people.

Their hunters were spread apart—like sentries on guard duty—and showed no inclination to move. Though a few of them were looking down at their phones, the rest seemed more diligent about their impromptu duty.

Crossing the street without being seen was impossible.

"This is bad," Cordelia said.

"Can we go around?"

"There's not enough time."

A car came to a screeching halt. Kyle got out and slammed the door. Laurel was nowhere in sight. It was strange seeing one without the other.

"Any sign of her?" he called out.

Head shakes up and down the street.

"Unbelievable! What are we paying you people for? She's just a girl, and she is somewhere in this village! She didn't just vanish!"

"He doesn't know I'm with you," Benji whispered.

"That's good."

"Yeah. It gives me an idea, actually."

"What idea?"

Benji took his phone out of his pocket, dropped it on the ground, and pummeled it with a nearby rock. The screen cracked in several places.

"Have you lost your mind?" Cordelia asked.

"That was painful," he said with a grimace, "but I need a prop to sell this. You'll have to get the last ghost on your own. Sorry."

Cordelia grabbed his arm.

"What are you going to do?"

"Something either really smart or really stupid. Let's find out!"

Benji ran out of the woods, making no attempt to avoid the employees who instantly closed in on him.

"Kyle!" he exclaimed. "I've been looking everywhere for you. Cordelia's here! We have to tell Laurel."

"We know," Kyle said with a suspicious gleam in his eyes.

"Oh, good," Benji replied, all innocence. "Have you found her yet?"

"No. Why don't you tell me where she is?"

Benji ignored the accusation in his voice. "I caught her taking pictures of the life windows. She said she was going to post them online. Even if people don't believe her about the ghosts, all those video screens are going to look pretty weird. Someone's bound to come investigate."

This sounded realistic enough to give Kyle pause.

"How many pictures did she take?" he asked.

"Don't worry," Benji said, clapping Kyle on the shoulder like they were best buddies. "I grabbed her phone and smashed it to pieces. I don't want anyone finding out about us. I'd lose my job!"

As proof, he showed Kyle the remnants of his own phone. That, more than anything, seemed to convince him that Benji was telling the truth.

"Good work," Kyle said. "Do you know where she is now?"

Benji turned his back to Cordelia and pointed straight ahead.

"She went that way. You know the stone house on Evergreen? There's a hole in the fence behind it. That's probably how she snuck in. My guess is she's going back the way she came—through the woods and onto the main road. Someone will probably pick her up there."

Cordelia stifled a laugh. There really was a hole in the fence. They had reported it months ago during their weekly inspections, but no one had ever fixed it. Before settling on their current plan, they had even toyed around with the idea of sneaking into the village that way.

In Kyle's mind, the mere existence of the hole must have somehow corroborated Benji's story, because all doubts vanished from his face. "Everyone, follow me!" he exclaimed. "We need to search the woods and get some people watching the main road!"

Staying there would have looked suspicious, so there was nothing Benji could do but get in the car with Kyle. The rest of the employees formed a caravan and followed him.

Within moments, the street was empty.

Cordelia was worried about Benji, but she didn't want to waste the opportunity he had given her. She sprinted into the blue house and quickly found the old man (who had moved from sea lions to penguins). The ghost catcher made a strange grinding noise when she started it up, like a garbage disposal trying to eat a spoon, but it quickly settled down and did its job.

"That wasn't funny," Cordelia said, taking the boo-tube.

She had just removed her spectercles when her phone dinged twice in quick succession. There were two texts from Dr. Roqueni.

Have Agnes. Know Benji is with Kyle. On way to get him.

Back exit. 15 min. Can you get there?

Cordelia quickly replied: YES ☺

The back exit was a gate that couldn't be entered from the outside but opened automatically for any car leaving Shady Rest. There was no guard or anyone else to stop them.

It was only five minutes away. Maybe less if she ran.

Heart thudding, Cordelia exited the house. The street was still empty, but for how long? Fortunately, she knew Shady Rest nearly as well as Shadow School by this point, so she was able to limit her time in the open by cutting through houses. In the front door, out the back. She didn't see a single car. *Did Kyle order everyone to look for me in the woods?* Cordelia imagined the entire staff, many in heels or dress shoes, stomping through the undergrowth. The dry-cleaning bills were going to be off the charts. If she hadn't been so stressed out, she would have laughed.

Later. Over ice cream.

With ten minutes to spare, she found herself on Willow Drive. The back exit was right over the next rise. If Cordelia remembered correctly, there was a thicket of overgrown shrubs that would provide a perfect hiding spot while she waited for Dr. Roqueni to arrive.

She checked to see if anyone was following her and saw the purple house, where the only remaining ghost in Shady Rest waited to be saved.

"No," Cordelia said. "Don't be an idiot. Back gate. Do the smart thing for once. The safe thing."

She started walking toward the exit, resolutely at first, then slower and slower.

Finally, she stopped.

It was strange that she had only one boo-tube left. That was kind of like fate, wasn't it? And how bad could the phantom inside the purple house really be? Worse than Gideon? Esmae? Dr. Gill? Cordelia found that hard to believe. It wasn't fair to save all those phantoms but leave this one behind. It had just been an innocent ghost before this cruel twist of fate. Life windows. Phantom cell. Those were the real terrors. This poor soul had already been punished enough.

While these thoughts ran through her mind, Cordelia had, almost without realizing it, been walking steadily toward the purple house. She now found herself standing on the front porch. It had been a long time since anyone had gotten this close to the entrance, and the wooden boards creaked beneath the unexpected weight. Cordelia put the duffel bag down and pulled the set of keys from her pocket. They were all clearly labeled with street names, save a single key with purple tape wound around its shaft. Cordelia slid this one into the keyhole.

"If this doesn't work, it's a sign I shouldn't be doing this," she said.

The lock clicked open with ease.

Cordelia opened the door. The hinges didn't squeak, but there was an airy sound like an exhalation of a long-held breath. Fixing her spectercles into place, Cordelia peeked inside. She could see the living room and most of the dining room. They were completely furnished. That baffled her for a moment, until she remembered that this had been the first house built in Shady Rest, and no doubt held a special place in Mr. Knox's heart. He would have wanted it to feel special.

There was no sign of the phantom.

Cordelia took a long breath. They had already accomplished so much. What was one more ghost?

Everything.

She picked up the duffel bag and entered the purple house.

20

The Purple House

Cordelia had the odd sensation that she was tres-
passing.

It looked as though the house might actually be
inhabited. Old magazines had been fanned across
the coffee table. The logs in the stone fireplace were
charred. There was even a coffee ring on one of the end
tables. After a moment's consideration, however, Cordelia realized that these were just meaningless details.
If someone had truly been living here, there wouldn't
be such a thick layer of dust on the furniture or cobwebs
hanging from the ceiling.

She checked her phone. Six minutes. That was
enough time to take a quick walkthrough of the house.

She decided to leave the ghost catcher in the living room for now. The duffel bag was cumbersome, and she didn't want to put herself in a position where she couldn't make a quick exit.

Just in case.

She started her search on the second floor. Mr. Knox had spared no expense. Every room looked like a postcard for a country inn. There was even a cozy library with fully stocked bookshelves. All the life windows were dark. After being bombarded by loud videos all day, the silence was eerie, though not unwelcome. Cordelia was tired of other people's memories.

There was no phantom upstairs, so she tried the first floor instead. Nothing. The house didn't have a basement, which was a nice change of pace.

The phantom was nowhere to be found.

She felt bad, but the safety of her friends was more important. Besides, there were still ghosts that had to get back to Shadow School before they burned through their boo-tubes. There was no more time to waste.

"Sorry. I tried."

As she bent down to pick up the duffel bag, Cordelia caught movement to her left. She spun around, heart racing, and saw a ghost beneath the dining room table. He was sitting with his knees bent and ankles crossed, just like the photo she had seen of him on

Facebook—though he had been sitting on a boulder that time.

Victor Price.

Cordelia knelt on the floor so she was eye level with the man. There was nothing about his appearance that made her believe he was anything other than a commonplace ghost. He was wearing khaki shorts with lots of pockets, a white T-shirt, and hiking shoes. If this had been Shadow School, she would have offered him a canteen.

"What are you doing here?"

The ghost didn't look at her, but Cordelia could tell he was aware of her presence. He pointed to the floor between them. A large dark stain had seeped into the wood. Cordelia didn't think it was cranberry juice.

"What happened here?" she asked, feeling very cold.

She looked back at the ghost and screamed. Victor's appearance had changed. The right side of his head was caved in and oozing blood, and his glasses hung askew from one ear, revealing cold and lifeless eyes.

He answered my question, Cordelia thought. *That's what happened here.*

This vision of Victor's death was gone as quickly as it came. The next moment, he was only a ghost again.

"Was there some kind of accident?" Cordelia asked.

Victor shook his head.

"Did someone . . . do this to you?"

Victor nodded.

"Laurel?"

Victor didn't need to nod. The answer could be found in the darkness that suddenly eclipsed his eyes.

Cordelia's phone dinged.

No doubt it was her friends, wondering where she was. She needed to leave. Things were serious now, in a very real way that went beyond ghosts and phantoms. Laurel was a murderer! A murderer!

If she caught them . . .

That wouldn't happen. Cordelia rose to her feet and picked up the duffel bag. Victor made no attempt to stop her, but his tormented face drove a stake through her heart. He was trapped here, in the place where his life ended, maybe reliving his final moments again and again.

She couldn't just leave him.

"Hold on, Victor," Cordelia said, setting the ghost catcher on the dining room floor. "You're coming with me."

The ghost saw the boo-tube in Cordelia's hand and began to shake his head violently.

"It's okay," Cordelia said. "It's just a—"

Victor flew upward through the dining room table

and plastered himself against the ceiling, where he could look down at her from a safe distance. Cordelia was momentarily baffled, then realized the problem. Victor had worked at Shady Rest. He knew what happened to ghosts who went into the boo-tubes.

"I know what you're thinking," Cordelia said in a placating voice. "But I'm not Laurel. I'm not going to turn you into a phantom. I'm going to take you to a place called Shadow School. It's the most wonderful place in the world. Think of it like an airport for ghosts. It'll get you where you're meant to be."

Victor remained pressed against the ceiling, but at least he had stopped shaking his head. He was listening.

"How would you like to spend eternity, Victor?" Cordelia asked. She thought about what little she had learned about him. "Hiking?"

He gave a surprised nod.

"Okay. Imagine a forest filled with plants you've never seen before and fantastic animals that let you ride them, and each view is more breathtaking than the last. That's where you can go, Victor. Or somewhere different, if you'd like. It's up to you. But you have to trust me."

Her phone dinged again.

"Sorry, Victor. I'd love to give you more time to

weigh the pros and cons, but I'm kind of on a tight schedule here!"

The ghost offered a hesitant nod and floated to the floor.

"You won't regret this," Cordelia said, attaching the boo-tube.

Her phone dinged again.

"My friends are probably freaking out," Cordelia said. "I better let them know I'm okay."

She picked up the phone and her heart fell. The texts weren't from her friends.

They were from Laurel.

I know you're in the purple house. Come out now.

Waiting for you outside.

I have your friends.

Cordelia walked to the front window in a daze. The entire staff of Shady Rest was standing in the street. She could see Benji and Agnes in the back seat of Dr. Roqueni's car, with the principal herself in the passenger's seat. Kyle was leaning against the hood, tossing the car keys from one hand to the other.

There were three light taps on the door, like an early morning visitor who didn't want to wake anyone else in the house. Cordelia didn't bother looking through the peephole. She knew who it was. *What's she waiting for?* The door wasn't locked. There was nothing to stop Laurel from marching into the house and dragging her out the door.

Except an angry ghost.

She's scared of Victor, Cordelia thought. *That's the real reason she keeps this house locked up—and to hide the evidence of her crime.*

Thinking frantically of a way she might be able to use that, Cordelia opened the door. Laurel stood on the front porch. The hatred on her face seemed like a living, breathing thing. Cordelia could practically feel it reach across the threshold and wrap its cold fingers around her neck.

"It's over," Laurel said. "But even though you tried to steal *everything* from me, I still don't want to see you get hurt. So first things first, Cordelia. Come outside before the phantom finds you."

"I'd trust a phantom over you any day."

Laurel smiled. It was as cold as a ghost's embrace.

"I know what you did," she said. "But don't worry. You can still make it right. From what I heard that old man tell my grandfather, your school is special, right? A smorgasbord of spirits. It should be easy enough to replace what you stole."

"So you can turn them into phantoms?"

"Why not? They're already dead. They won't know the difference."

"Is that what you really think? You don't understand ghosts at all. They're helpless, Laurel. You can't just—"

"Ugh! You sound just like Grandpa. He spent his entire life helping the helpless. And when he died, do you know how much money he left me? Nothing. Nada. Zilch. Apparently all those endangered animals and rain forests and starving people were more important that his own *granddaughter.*"

"He left you Shady Rest. That's a treasure far more valuable than money. It shows how much he loved you."

A flicker of regret crossed Laurel's eyes, like a lightning bug on a starless night. After it had passed, only darkness remained.

"Well, that was his mistake. Because I'm going to use this stupid place to recoup all the money that should have been mine—and you're going to help me do it. Step outside, Cordelia."

"What if I say no? Are you going to kill me like you killed Victor?"

The color drained from Laurel's face. When she spoke again it was at a whisper. She didn't want the people standing in the street to hear her.

"Don't be ridiculous. I never touched him."

"You do remember that I see ghosts, right? Victor showed me the bloodstains on the floor."

Laurel craned her head to look past Cordelia. "You saw him?" she asked with a trembling voice.

"He's right there," Cordelia said. She turned around, meaning to indicate the dining room, and jumped in surprise. Victor was in the hallway behind her, hovering a few inches off the floor. He was pointing at Laurel.

"It wasn't my fault," Laurel said, moving as close to the threshold as she dared. "Victor wanted more money. He threatened to tell my grandfather what we were doing to the ghosts if I didn't pay him. Can you imagine? After everything I did for him, he dared to *blackmail* me? My grandfather would have cut me out of the will. I would have lost everything! So I hit him with the closest thing at hand: a boo-tube. They're surprisingly heavy, you know."

"I know," Cordelia said.

"Here's the good news, Cordelia," Laurel said. "I won't hurt you. Or Benji. I lied when I said I could find someone else with the Sight. It's incredibly rare. So you two lovebirds can rest assured that no harm will ever come to you. But your parents? Benji's sisters? Agnes? They're all fair game, as far as I'm concerned. I will do whatever it takes. You understand? Now get out of that house before I come in there and get you!"

She felt a cold presence behind her. Victor, still floating, was looking over her shoulder, straight at Laurel. The whites of his eyes had turned red.

"I think you should stay out there," Cordelia said.

Laurel scoffed. Her patience was beginning to fray.

"Don't tell me what to do. You think Victor will protect you? Please. I bet I can grab you before he even knows I'm there. Unless . . ." Laurel looked past Cordelia at the ghost catcher. The boo-tube was still sticking out of it. "Oh, you clever girl! Victor isn't even in the house anymore, is he? You already captured him."

"Not yet. He's right behind me."

Laurel took a step closer. She raised a foot teasingly over the threshold.

"Don't," Cordelia said.

"Why should I believe you? You've done nothing but lie to me. You're alone. I know it!"

With a final burst of courage, Laurel leaped into the house. She paused for a moment, eyes wide, waiting for something to happen. When nothing did, she smiled with satisfaction and grabbed Cordelia's arm.

"Let's get to this school of yours," she said, yanking Cordelia across the floor. "You have a lot of ghosts to catch."

The front door slammed shut. Laurel's face suddenly appeared on all the life windows. She was staring down at a bloody boo-tube with a surprised look on her face. The memory went dark, then repeated. Again. And again.

It was Victor's last sight before he closed his eyes forever.

"Help!" Laurel screamed. She tried the doorknob and immediately yanked her hand away. Her fingers were frozen into a misshapen claw.

"Stop it, Victor," Cordelia called out, looking left and right. She had no idea where the ghost had gone. "This isn't you."

The light in the house grew dimmer as Victor reappeared. Cordelia had met all kinds of spirits during the past three years, but this was her first encounter with a vengeful ghost. She hoped it would be her last. Victor's eyes were entirely red, and all other facial features—nose, mouth, ears—had simply vanished. It was as though all the humanity had been shaved from his face, leaving only his desire for revenge.

The ghost's fingers whipped around Laurel's neck like tentacles and raised her off the floor. Cordelia knew what Laurel had done was wrong, but that didn't make this right. She grabbed the ghost catcher and placed it at Victor's feet. As the ghost leaned forward, drinking in Laurel's final moments with his bloodred eyes, Cordelia pressed the doorbell.

Victor turned into mist.

It took Laurel a solid minute before her breathing steadied. She rose to a sitting position and gave Cordelia a bewildered look.

"You saved me," she said.

"I saved Victor. You just happened to be there."

Laurel managed a wry grin. "Go. All of you. Before I change my mind."

Smoke was rising from the ghost catcher. The black box had cracked in two, and the cottage was a charred mess, like the aftermath of a fire. It was clear that the machine had caught its last ghost. Cordelia gave it an affectionate pat and removed Victor's boo-tube from the nozzle.

His mist was layered in orange and violet, like a sunset.

21

Graduation

Although eighth-grade graduation was usually held in the auditorium, Dr. Roqueni had decided to have it outside this year. Chairs had already been set up on the front lawn, along with two large tents for refreshments afterward. There was a slight chance of thunderstorms later in the afternoon, but right now the sky was a brilliant shade of blue.

Inside the school, Cordelia paced back and forth across the mirror gallery, wringing her hands. She was wearing a polka-dotted dress that her mother had bought her for the occasion. Soon she would have to don her graduation robe and head outside, but there was something important she needed to do first. She only hoped she could find the courage to see it through to the end.

"I figured I'd find you here," Dr. Roqueni said, eyeing the two chairs in the center of the room—and what lay upon them. "Nervous?"

"More than you can imagine."

"You'll be fine. I'm surprised you didn't bring your sketchbook, just in case you see any ghosts while you wait."

"I'm going to focus on landscapes for a while. Mr. Keene says I should expand my repertoire before I start the advanced class at Cavendish."

"Smart. I'm glad you finally got your portfolio together."

"Me too."

The week after their final trip to Shady Rest, Cordelia had gathered her notebooks and gone to see the art teacher. Mr. Keene had been blown away by her drawings of the ghosts. He had even framed the sketch of Esmae and hung it in his classroom to "inspire future students."

Dr. Roqueni's face grew serious.

"Laurel confessed to the police," she said. "That may help her in the end."

"I hope so. What's going to happen to Shady Rest?"

"It was just purchased by a developer. You won't

believe what they're turning it into."

"What?"

"A retirement community."

Their laughter reverberated through the mirror gallery.

"I believe I owe you the second part of your gift," Dr. Roqueni said.

She handed Cordelia a red drawstring bag. Inside was a key.

"It opens the main door of Shadow School," Dr. Roqueni said. "I know you won't be a student here anymore. But I want you to think of this as a second home. You'll always be welcome here."

Cordelia threw her arms around the principal and gave her a giant hug. "Thank you. For everything."

As they pulled apart, Cordelia's parents entered the room.

"We got your grandparents all settled," Mr. Liu said. "They'll save seats for us. Third row, center!"

"Your father is very excited," Mrs. Liu said, patting his arm.

"I better head down and do my principal thing," Dr. Roqueni said. She stopped to shake hands with Mr. and Mrs. Liu. "You have an amazing daughter. I'm going to miss her."

"Thank you," said Mrs. Liu. "Cordelia has loved

her time here. This is clearly a very special school."

"That it is," said Dr. Roqueni.

Mr. and Mrs. Liu turned toward their daughter. As they did, the ghost of an old woman floated into the room. She was lying on her back with her arms behind her head, as though chilling on a pool raft.

Perfect timing, Cordelia thought.

"Why did you want to meet up here?" Mr. Liu asked.

Cordelia changed the position of the chairs so they were facing the ghost. "Come sit down," she said, picking up the two pairs of spectercles. "There's something I want to show you."

The speeches were short, and no one tripped over their robes, which was really all you could ask for in a graduation ceremony. Afterward, everyone gathered beneath the tents for cookies and lukewarm lemonade. When Cordelia, Benji, and Agnes got tired of smiling for photos, they snuck over to the playground. It had been a long time since they'd sat on the swings, but it felt like the right thing to do.

"How did your parents take it?" Agnes asked.

"They're still processing," Cordelia said. "Ask me again next week. How about yours?"

"Surprisingly well," Benji said. "Apparently my

bisabuela could see ghosts. A few of my cousins too."

"Look at that. It's like a Núñez family tradition."

"I don't think my parents believed me," Agnes said.

"How do you know?" Benji asked.

"Because they said, 'We don't believe you.'"

"You could use the spectercles like I did," suggested Cordelia.

"Nah," Agnes said. "I think I'll keep this secret to myself. Their loss."

Benji heard his name and looked toward the parking lot. His parents and three sisters were waving in his direction. Sofia spotted Cordelia and began to make kissy faces in their direction.

"I gotta run," Benji said. "My dad made reservations at some fancy restaurant for lunch."

"I should probably go too," Cordelia said. She squeezed Benji's hand. "What time's the movie tonight?"

"It depends. Seven for the funny one or eight for the scary one. Which one do you want to see?"

"Do you even have to ask?"

"Hey!" Agnes exclaimed. "Do you guys want to make it a double date?"

Cordelia gasped. "Does this mean you've finally made a decision? Who's the lucky winner? Mark or Kedar?"

"Colton!"

"Colton?"

"I met him at the ice cream shop last week!"

"All right, then," Cordelia said, laughing. "I would love to meet him. What kind of science does he like?"

"Oh, he's not really into science. Or school." A dreamy look came into Agnes's eyes. "Colton plays the *guitar*!"

"Oh boy," Benji said.

They crossed the front lawn, joining the exodus of students and parents headed toward the front gate. Cordelia stopped for one last look at the school and gasped with delight.

There were ghosts standing at every window.

She recognized them all. At one point or another, she had helped every one of them. Here the surfer whose Brightkey had been a pair of earplugs, there the old woman who had wanted a broom. Cordelia saw the first ghost she had ever freed, a bearded man who dreamed of reading his newspaper forever, and far too many joggers. And finally, arm-in-arm with a little trick-or-treater that Cordelia had once taunted with a chocolate bar, she saw Mr. Derleth's son, Owen. He gave her a cheerful wave.

"Goodbye," Cordelia said.

She caught up with her friends and threw her arms around their shoulders. They passed through the gate together.

Acknowledgments

Thank you, readers, young and old, who took this journey with Cordelia, Benji, and Agnes. Without you, I'm just some dude typing unread manuscripts in his basement.

I want to express my sincere gratitude to my agent, Alexandra Machinist, who has been there since the beginning and never ceases to amaze. Also, I'd like to thank my foreign rights agent, Roxane Edouard, and my film agent, Josie Freedman. They really are the best.

Katherine Tegen, my editor, continues to wow me with her insight. It's actually a little creepy. But I like creepy, so that's okay.

There is a host of other people to thank: Sara Schonfeld, Petur Antonsson, Jennifer Sheridan,

Audrey Churchward, Robert Imfeld, Mabel Hsu, Kim Mai Guest, Gweneth Morton, Mark Rifkin, and Shona McCarthy. As a proud grammar nerd (just ask my students), I must bow to the copyediting wizardry of Maya Myers, who patiently cleaned up my blunders and continuity errors. ("So, you said it was summer two paragraphs ago, but now it's snowing . . .")

If I left anyone out, I guarantee that your name is here—you just need spectercles to see it.

Thanks to Jess and Linds for all the entertaining texts. I probably would have finished the books faster if you didn't help me procrastinate so much, but it was totally worth it.

To our kids, Jack, Logan, and Colin: I'm sorry I had to work so much and didn't have time to play *Super Smash Bros.* with you. On the other hand, I would have just embarrassed myself, so maybe it's for the best.

And, finally, my everlasting love and gratitude to my wife, Yeeshing. My Bright is any place you are.